I0645075

"Phase Two…The time you've always wanted." The slogan from a magnetic Heron Company advertisement piques college student Avery Jenson's interest. She innocently selects Heron and their mysterious Phase Two plans as a topic for her college paper but quickly learns that the company and plan holders are very tight-lipped regarding Heron's services. She presses on and soon her world collides with Katie, a single mother, who sought a Phase Two plan for her daughter but was denied. Katie's earth-shattering experience with the company left her charged up and posed to take action. The two unlikely partners believe that there is something more sinister at work than immediately apparent, and Avery quickly realizes that this is going to be far more than a simple research paper—they have a vital mission to carry out.

PHASE TWO

A Novel by

Sandra Sikonia

A Black Opal Books Publication

For Cameron

Chapter 1

The TV flickered in the background as Avery sat at the table with books and papers scattered in front of her. She tried to organize her study schedule for her first year of college, but her mind was preoccupied with the semester-long research project she'd been assigned. She was supposed to write the longest paper of her life on the social ramifications of a new product or technology but had no idea where to start. She was thankful to be relieved from this dilemma temporarily when the doorbell rang.

"Ready to watch *Beachside*?" Sarah said the moment Avery answered the door.

"Ugh, I want to be able to just relax and enjoy it, but I am super stressed," Avery admitted. "I feel like I'm barely going to be able to pay attention. I really think I made a big mistake."

"What do you mean?"

"I signed up for this stupid five-credit class, Science and Society, but they assigned this mega-long research project." Avery sighed. "I'm already stuck."

Sarah laughed like only a best friend could do at a

moment like this. "You're just being dramatic. What's the problem?"

"We have to 'find a scientific company making an innovative breakthrough' and research it," Avery read from the syllabus. "Then we have to write a twenty-page paper about it and the 'implications for society.' I have to submit the name of my company by midnight."

"Wow, that does sound kind of tough," Sarah admitted. "But I bet once you stop stressing about the deadline, the rest will come to you. I feel like the brain can't work properly when it's so stressed out," she said, half trying to help calm Avery down and half trying to get Avery as psyched about *Beachside* as she was. "Blow that off for now. I can help you brainstorm later."

"I don't know. I'm seriously freaking out about this project," Avery said. "You know my mother expects me to do well here. Otherwise, she wouldn't have agreed to let me get an off-campus apartment." She was still a little shocked that her mother had permitted this kind of freedom, but they both knew Avery would gain control of her trust fund soon. "I have to show her I can be responsible for myself."

"But you're still not going to get the answer stressing over it," Sarah said, in that reasonable tone that could convince Avery of anything.

"But I need to think of something really cool and new. Otherwise, this project is going to be torture."

"How do you even find out about stuff like that?" Sarah asked.

"I have no idea. I think they were talking about that in class, but I wasn't paying much attention. It was the day I got that card."

"Oh right, the one from your dad?"

"He is not my dad!" Avery couldn't believe Sarah would use that word to refer to the man.

"Come on, Avery. Reuben was just congratulating you for getting into this school. At least he's trying to reconnect. And he set up that trust fund for you and all. That was nice."

"You don't get it. You know he walked out on us the week I started first grade. And what? Now he's trying to come back into my life weeks after I start college? I already have a dad in Marshall, thank you. Marshall's the one who raised me. I don't need Reuben."

"Okay, okay, I get it. It makes total sense. You were worked up about the card, so you weren't paying much attention in class when they talked about how to find a company. But you took detailed notes, right?" Somehow Sarah even managed to sound serious.

It took a beat, but finally, Avery let out a breath, letting her anger fade. She let out a small laugh. "I don't think I even had a pen that day. I was running late."

"You're doing a bang-up job of proving you can be responsible," Sarah said. "So what kind of handouts did they give?"

"There's all this stuff about how to use the library."

"Why go through all that? Just type something in the search bar."

"I tried that already." Avery groaned. "You should see what kind of stuff comes up. I gave up on about the fifth page. There was nothing really good."

"Well, you can't go to the library right now anyway," Sarah said.

"Why not?"

"Duh, *Beachside* is about to come on. We have, like, a minute, before it starts, and this is going to be a good one. Stuff was about to go down between Maria and Duke, I think."

"Right, I forgot! It did end kind of crazy last week." Avery recalled trying to rally herself for the show. She not only knew that Sarah was right, and it wouldn't kill her to relax a little, but watching *Beachside* with Sarah had become somewhat of a tradition for the girls since their days in prep school where they had become friends.

"It is going to be a good one. Thanks for letting us watch here this week. My mom is having yet another one of her dinner parties, and it's good to get out of there for a bit," Sarah said.

"Totally. I hear you." As Avery finished her words she glanced over at the TV and noticed one of the characters from *Beachside* on the screen and tapped Sarah, pointing and indicting it was time.

"Yessss, it's starting."

Avery grabbed her water and the remote from the table, and the girls hustled over to the couch and settled in to watch. The two were a little annoyed when they realized what was just being played was only a teaser, and now they would have to suffer through a whole series of stupid advertisements before the good stuff with Maria and Duke. Sarah took this as a cue to get in a quick bathroom break before the show actually started. She jumped up and hustled to the bathroom, trying to be quick to ensure she didn't miss anything.

Avery wasn't really paying much attention to the images flickering past while Sarah was away but something on the screen caught her attention and caused her to refocus.

It was a commercial she'd seen several times before. For some reason, it always pulled her in. The background was sky-colored. A slender woman in her late forties or early fifties dressed in a crisp business suit stood in the foreground. She had short brown hair fashioned into a professional-looking style with it slicked back securely in place behind the ears.

She spoke in a slow, soothing, almost captivating

tone. "Are there a few more things you'd like to do in your life? More time you'd like to spend with your loved ones?"

The image changed to show people engaged in various activities. A man and woman hiking, grandparents playing with their grandchildren, several generations of a happy family gathered around the covered porch of a large house.

"With Phase Two technology, it's now possible to ensure you'll have a chance to enjoy the kind of life you've always dreamed of with no personal risk. Call us to schedule an initial consultation."

The women gave a graceful wave of her hand and then eased out of the scene as the company name, logo, and contact information slid to the center from the opposite side.

"Phase Two is now available exclusively from the Heron Company," an invisible male announcer said. "Phase Two…the time you always wanted."

Sarah hurried back into the living room and onto the couch, "Did I miss anything? Has it started yet?"

"No," Avery replied somewhat distracted as she grabbed her computer. Curious, she typed *Heron Company* into the search engine.

Sarah sighed and said, "I thought you were taking a break."

"I am. I mean, I am going to. I just want to look at something really fast."

"Okay, you better hurry though."

When she found the page, Avery saw the same calming blue background with wistful clouds floating around and the company's tagline, *The time you always wanted.* The page offered an embedded video, with that same woman from the commercial, explaining that the Heron Company was honored to offer their clients this amazing opportunity, thanks to significant breakthroughs in current technology. There was something about living the life of your dreams but not much information about how the company delivered.

A ping of energy zipped through her system as Avery realized whatever they were doing had to be scientifically based and, since not even their website outlined what it was, it had to be innovative. With relief, she logged into her Science and Society class webpage and filled out the form indicating the focus of her research project. She could hear the voices of Maria and Duke just as she shut her computer.

Chapter 2

Up until about two and a half years ago or so, Katie Sullivan had been happy with her life. True, her ex-husband just couldn't take the pressure of being a parent, which made her a single mom with a lot of bills and responsibilities, but she was in a pretty good spot with a dependable job and a stable home. She and her daughter, Ella, were making it.

Katie knew she was lucky to have a kid like Ella. At only age nine, she helped around the house, did well in school, and actually liked attending classes. People were always surprised at Ella's young age because of the way she interacted with adults.

Katie supported Ella, but in her own way, Ella supported Katie. They were a team.

Everything changed the day Ella was diagnosed with a rare form of leukemia. A set of words that were completely foreign to Katie three years ago, they now lived and breathed every day—Philadelphia chromosome-type Acute Lymphoblastic Leukemia.

Their lives were uprooted as Ella underwent aggressive cancer treatment, followed by almost two years now of chemotherapy and other treatments to try to kill off what remained of the cancer cells.

Ella illness severely tested Katie's strength. Days were filled with phone calls to doctors, emails, looking up information on the internet, calling an increasingly distant family, spending time at the hospital with Ella, chemotherapy, bone marrow transplants, holding Ella through the more negative effects of the chemo and, of course, somehow finding time to keep her job. All the treatments and demands proved to be too much for Ella's already non-committed father, and he'd disappeared entirely within the first year. Katie tried really hard to keep her composure, but it was a challenge every day.

It was only Thursday, and Katie was already feeling worn down. The reports had not come in as expected, her boss needed a presentation yesterday, and Ella was kept in the hospital overnight. Katie placed the latest stack of files on her desk and sat for a breather when her cell phone rang with the tone reserved only for Ella's doctor.

"Ms. Sullivan. This is Dr. Feinberg."

"Yes?" Katie said, a little shaky with anxiety about the unscheduled call. After all, she was already scheduled to pick Ella up after work.

"I have some news about Ella. I would like to sit down with you before you pick her up."

"Of course," she said. "I'll come in now. Will you be available around three?"

"Just tell the receptionist in Ella's wing to page me when you arrive."

Katie frantically grabbed for her purse, shuffled through some papers, turned off her computer, and headed toward the door. Her fingers were shaking as she reached to press the elevator button.

What did Dr. Feinberg have to say, and why did he want to say it in person instead of on the phone? Was it bad news? It had to be. Why else wouldn't he have told her? Tears started to form behind her eyes before Katie checked herself.

Calm down, Katie. Don't get ahead of things, she told herself. *Just go to the hospital, meet with Dr. Feinberg, find out what he has to say, and go from there.*

When she reached the car, she dug through her purse to find her keys, getting frustrated. She couldn't find them in the mess of paraphernalia she always carried for Ella. She dumped out her entire bag on the parking garage's floor and groaned as she fanned through the mess of items on the concrete. Once she found the keys hidden under a tangle of travel games to keep Ella entertained during infusions, tissues to clean up after her when she got sick, and a headscarf in case Ella forgot a hat, Katie shoveled everything back into her bag and tossed her purse over her shoulder into the backseat of the car, wishing she had the right kind of purse without all the tools needed to care for a cancer patient.

Mostly, she just wished Ella could get well, and with that thought, Katie headed off to the hospital with her mind racing.

She was a little winded when she reached reception, but she was able to tell the receptionist, Gail, that Dr. Feinberg wanted to meet with her.

Gail looked down and up at Katie. "You may go to his office," she said in a voice that revealed nothing.

Dr. Feinberg met Katie at his door, shaking her hand and gesturing her in before closing the door behind her.

"Why don't you have a seat, Ms. Sullivan, so we can chat?"

Katie could feel the pulse in her neck jump up a notch at his words and her knees just about buckled of their own accord before she reached the chair. *Why does he want me to sit down? Have I always sat down when we talked about Ella?* She told herself to calm down. *Just sit, breathe, and listen to what he has to say,* she thought.

Dr. Feinberg proceeded, "Ms. Sullivan, we did a battery of testing and have concluded that Ella's leukemia should be in remission."

Katie almost couldn't breathe. She had been dreaming of this day. But the doctor hadn't said it was. He had said *should be.*

"What do you mean?" she asked.

"Ideally, I'd like to keep her on her treatment plan for another six months just to be sure," Dr. Feinberg said, looking a little defeated. "However, it seems Ella's already reached your insurance company's lifetime maximum coverage. I wanted to talk with you in private in case you might have another source of funding."

Katie was stunned. Was that even legal to allow the insurance company to determine the course of treatment? She'd kept an eye on the invoices. She knew, ballpark, how much it would cost to keep Ella's treatment going for another six months. She didn't make that kind of money. She searched her brain for other options and was coming up with nothing. Still in shock, Katie told the doctor the truth. "There's no way I can afford it on my own, and I don't have much family to turn to. I am confused. Are you saying it's necessary or ideal for her to continue?"

With a sad nod of his head, the doctor acknowledged Katie's financial limitations before responding to her question. "I am optimistic that Ella's leukemia is gone. We could not find any trace of it in our tests, which means it is no longer necessary for her to continue treatments. We will continue to keep an eye on her."

"What are you saying?" Katie asked.

"Among other things that there are some advantages to her stopping treatment at this time," he said. "Her body can begin to heal from the negative effects of the medication. And she can return to living a normal life without suffering from the side effects." The doctor struggled back up to his feet and motioned Katie ahead of him toward the door. "She should be fine, but you may want to investigate some additional coverage options in case there is a need in the future."

Together they walked back down the hallway to Ella's room.

While Katie bent to give her daughter a welcome hug, Dr. Feinberg caught up on Ella's charts.

"Ella, you are looking well. How are you feeling this afternoon?" he asked her.

"Pretty good," she replied.

Dr. Feinberg then explained, "Ella, I was just telling your mom that your cancer is gone now."

Katie turned and looked at Ella, who was smiling.

"Mommy, now things can go back to how they were before."

Katie wasn't sure what parts she meant, but it didn't really matter. "Yes, baby, they can." She looked at Dr. Feinberg.

Dr. Feinberg understood and ran his hand through his thick gray hair as he clarified, "Ella is going to take some time to regain her strength, but she will get it back in time. We will work on the discharge paperwork for the morning. She will have to continue to return for regular checkups. There is always a chance for the cancer to reappear, so if that were to occur, we would want to catch it as early as possible."

Katie said she understood. As she was taking this all in, she glanced down for a moment and noticed a silver bracelet clasped around Dr. Feinberg's pale wrist. *Phase Two* was engraved into the flat silver plate that looked strikingly like a fancy medical alert bracelet.

She surprised herself by asking, "What *is* Phase Two? I have seen those commercials."

Oddly, Dr. Feinberg ignored her question entirely. Instead, he redirected as he stretched out his hand, the one with the bracelet, and said, "Congratulations." He did the same to Ella. As he shuffled out the door, he mentioned, "Gail will be in with your discharge papers shortly."

What a strange response. Make that non-response. Katie couldn't help but wonder why he had been dismissive when she asked about Phase Two.

Ella needed to spend one last night in the hospital, and Katie wanted to make sure she had time to do a thorough house cleaning to ensure the house was just perfect prior to Ella arriving home. After working through the paperwork with Gail and chatting some with Ella, she said, "I will be back first thing in the morning. Sleep well. I love you."

Katie headed out of the hospital and back to the parking garage. When she arrived at the hospital earlier, her body had been tense and her mind racing, wondering what Dr. Feinberg might say. Now she was elated, but her mind was still in turmoil.

Katie was exhausted. It was almost eleven at night, but she was still running on adrenaline. After she finished cleaning up and getting Ella's room together, she settled on the couch with the laptop to wind down for the evening so she could get some rest and be ready for the big day. While she was catching up on some email and other business, a small advertisement embedded in her page caught her eye. It was for Phase Two. She remembered seeing Dr. Feinberg's bracelet and wondering about his reaction to her questioning. She clicked.

When she arrived at the Phase Two website, it looked just like the advertisements on TV. *The time you have always wanted* was a slogan that appeared prominently and was central to any message provided by the video clips. On one page, she saw the fine print, *Time provided is ten years beyond original client departure date.*

Ten years! thought Katie. It was a little uncomfortable to see departure date used that way, seemingly a euphemism for death. Katie had spent the past two and a half years dreaming of Ella getting a chance to be a normal kid again. Now Ella had that chance, and while Katie wasn't sure if this Phase Two thing was legitimate, she was willing to find out if it meant the possibility of securing Ella's future. She filled out the online application for a consultation and sent it in. When she finally shut the laptop, it was past midnight.

Katie headed out the next morning well before Ella's eight a.m. discharge time so she could stop at the grocery to pick up a balloon. She settled on one that said: *Congratulations* and had many different colored cartoonish daisies surrounding the word. As she waited her turn, another customer stepped up beside her, facing the customer service counter. Out of the corner of her eye, Katie noticed the woman was wearing the same silver Phase Two bracelet Dr. Feinberg had been wearing the day before.

The customer service person became available but turned his attention to the woman with the bracelet next to Katie first, even though it was clear Katie had been waiting longer.

Katie was annoyed. She was in a good mood with Ella coming home, and she didn't have the energy to get into it with these two, so she decided to let it go. Though as she waited, she replayed the scenario in her head. She was there first. Why did the man ignore her and help the other woman? Was it an honest mistake? Should she say something? Was it something to do with that bracelet? It did seem like he glanced at it. Her thoughts were inter-rupted.

"Ma'am, what can I do for you?"

Once Katie had the balloon, she headed off to the hospital. When she arrived at the hospital, with balloon in hand, Ella was with Gail, who was guiding her into a wheelchair. The three headed toward the exit, but when they reached the door, they all looked at one another. Tears pricked at Katie's eyes, as she knew what was really happening here. They were each realizing it was actually time for Ella to go home for good.

Gail was the first to say something. "Young lady, it was an absolute delight getting to know you." She was tearing up but continued. "We are all very happy for you and wish you the very best."

"Thank you for everything," Ella said. "I'll miss you."

Gail leaned down and hugged her. When Gail stood back up, she looked at Katie. "Well, I guess this is it. Congratulations."

They hugged as well, and Katie whispered, "I cannot thank you enough," into Gail's ear.

"You are very welcome, dear." Gail gently helped Ella into Katie's car. "Goodbye, you two," she said, and slowly turned back to the hospital with the wheelchair.

It was official. Katie and Ella headed home and whatever the future might hold.

Chapter 3

"Maybe I should just drop the class," Avery moaned at Sarah a week or so after turning in her chosen company name for the big Science and Society paper.

"That's not like you to give up like that." Sarah took another bite of her deli sandwich, obviously waiting for Avery to explain.

"I can't find anything out about the company," Avery said. "I've searched every site I can find that mentions it, read every newspaper article and press release, and still all I can figure out is that I think they've figured out some way to give people ten extra years of life somehow."

"Really?" Sarah raised an eyebrow. "It seems like that would have been kind of big news. What's the company name?"

"I know, right? The Heron Company. Have you ever heard of it?"

"No, I don't think so. Wait, they're the ones with the sky commercials, right?"

Avery nodded.

"Nope, that's about all I know about them," Sarah said. "But there must be something online somewhere."

"There is. I found a customer forum, but most of the people who post are like me, just trying to find out some answers about what the company is actually doing. A couple are members and talk about how the process is so easy and 'non-invasive,' but they don't tell you what they did. There's even people who say they're 'in it' which is apparently some kind of catch phrase to say that they're already in their ten-year terms, whatever that means."

"Nobody says what actually happens, even with people asking?"

"Nope. It's really strange. All they say is if you're curious, you should make an appointment with the company."

"Are you going to do that?" Sarah said in a way that implied she already assumed the answer would be a definite no.

Avery wasn't sure about setting an appointment to talk with a Phase Two representative. She had a strong feeling they would pressure her into buying something, but she wanted to know more about what they did so she could write the paper and pass her class. Avery was determined to start her college career off on the right foot and show herself, and her mother, she could be a successful independent young woman. Besides, she signed up for this Science and Society class, in part because it sounded interesting, so she was set on getting something positive out of it, despite the rough start.

"Well, there's this seminar thing I saw they are offering," she said, instead of answering the question. "I might be able to figure out what I need to know from there, but it's not for a while. I was really hoping to get a jump start on this thing."

"Where is it?" Sarah asked, looking sideways at her friend.

"I know, you're thinking I'm going to be dragging you to some crazy wild part of town," Avery said with a smile. She'd always been the more adventurous one, which frequently got them into trouble at prep school. "It's at the Easton-Downtown conference center. Will you come with me? I really feel like I need this on the books in case I keep struggling with this project."

"I don't know. Will there be chocolate cake?"

"Come on. I'll buy you dessert after if there isn't."

"You know how to tempt me."

"Great! I'll remind you when it's coming up."

Avery was relieved she wouldn't have to go alone when the time came. Living so far away from her family, she and Sarah were as close as sisters, and she knew Sarah would never abandon her.

While Avery's parents lived some distance away, Sarah's mother was now within easy driving distance, which made it easy for her mother to insist she attend the never-ending dinner parties Sarah loathed. Sometimes Avery wished her own mother were so insistent that they spend some quality time together, but then she reminded herself of the true nature of Sarah's relationship with her mother, a continuous cycle of power plays, and Avery felt glad she at least had a mother she could still talk to.

"Just don't get me caught up in any crazy cult movement or anything," Sarah joked. "My mother would never forgive you."

They laughed as they parted ways, each heading to different parts of the college campus for afternoon classes. When Avery got home later that evening, she pulled up the Heron Company's website and filled in the requisite form to indicate she planned to attend the seminar and bring a guest. Once her application was accepted, she was redirected to a screen formatted for printing tickets for entry, and she dutifully pushed the button.

Would they kick me out if I showed up without this? she wondered but felt pretty confident this was just another trick played by companies like this one. They made it seem like they were all exclusive and everything but then turned out to be just as gimmicky as the next guy.

Thinking about gimmicky salesmen reminded Avery of her mother's description of her biological father Reuben, whom she insisted was "just another fancy salesman with more flash than substance." After Reuben left, her mom found someone much more stable to be her father in Marshall. Maybe she would have some useful advice for how Avery could find the answers she was looking for.

"So, Mom, have you ever heard of the Heron Company?" she asked as soon as was appropriate after calling her mother unexpectedly.

"Heron Company? I don't think so, dear. Who are they?"

"You know, the company that sells the Phase Two thing," she said.

"Oh yes, I have seen those commercials. Looks like a lot of flash to me."

"I thought you'd say that."

"Avery, you are not getting involved with that company, are you?"

"Sarah and I are going to check it out. Actually, we're attending one of their upcoming seminars. I just signed us up."

"Ohhh…" Avery's mom said, not even trying to hide the skepticism in her voice. "Why are you girls doing that?"

Avery thought for a moment about telling her mother the true reason she was investigating the company, because of her class project, but something about her mother's tone irritated her, as if Avery weren't old enough to take care of herself.

"Why shouldn't we go?" she said instead. "We are curious about what they do."

"Well, Avery, you know many of these kinds of companies are just looking to take advantage of people with idealistic dreams."

"You don't even know what they do. How can you accuse them of that?" Avery couldn't believe she was defending a company she didn't know anything about, but that was the kind of logic that conversations with her mother always seemed to bring out.

"Dear, you know you tend to buy into things a bit too quickly. I'm worried these people will take advantage of you. You really need to learn a bit more discretion before you expose yourself to these risks."

"What risks, Mom? I'm just going to a seminar with Sarah."

"I'm worried about you attending that liberal college. Maybe it's too open to new ideas. That company provides no information in their ads. I'm sure they're up to no good, and I'm certain I don't want you involved."

"You can't keep me isolated forever, Mother." Avery tried hard to keep her anger in check. She hated it when her mother insisted on treating her like a child. "Wouldn't you say it's better for me to explore 'new ideas' now and learn how to evaluate them for myself? You didn't even remember that company before I mentioned it to you, and yet you accuse me of being too hasty."

"Now, Avery, don't get yourself worked up," her mother tried to interject.

"I'm not a child anymore, in case you hadn't noticed. You can't keep me from going. There are no rules against it."

"Okay, Avery."

Avery took some satisfaction in hearing the note of defeat and helplessness in her mother's voice.

"Where is this seminar you're going to?"

"The Easton."

"Isn't that the beautiful hotel in downtown, the one with the gold fountain?"

"That's the one."

"Well, at least they chose a classy venue. Still, you'll be downtown. Make sure when you girls go that you take your pepper spray, and don't wander too far from the crowds."

"Mom, I'm completely capable of taking care of myself in the city. Or did you forget I've been learning to take care of myself since back in boarding school?"

Avery could almost hear her mom wince at that last one, but when would the woman learn to stop telling her what to do and treating her like a child?

"Okay, well, be careful," her mom said, adopting a more conciliatory tone. "You know I love you, right?"

"I know it," Avery said, suddenly feeling a little ashamed of herself. Maybe she lost her patience with her mom a little too often "I love you, too," she added with feeling.

"Don't get sucked into some scam, dear."

"We'll be careful," Avery said.

"Good. I love you."

"Love you, too. Night."

Chapter 4

Over the next two days, Ella and her mother went to the aquarium together, had a picnic, went to the movies, and shared some wonderful meals, including lasagna, which was Ella's favorite. Ella loved to help in the kitchen, so cooking was a really fun way to spend time together.

Over dinner, they discussed school. Ella was excited to get her life back to the way it had been before, but she was nervous about what that might mean. "So I won't have to sit out of PE anymore?" she asked.

Even though Katie worried a bit about Ella's strength, she knew it was good for her to be busy and acting like a healthy kid again.

"Tell you what. We'll call the school first thing in the morning and talk with Ms. Jamie about what's our best plan," Katie suggested.

"Okay, Mom," Ella said.

In the morning, Katie let Ella sleep while she checked her email.

Thank you for your interest in The Heron Company. We have received your inquiry and information. We would like you to attend an informational appointment and interview on Wednesday at 11:00 A.M. If you have any questions or need to schedule this appointment for another time, please contact Heron Company's customer service. Due to our high demand, it may take longer to reschedule your visit. During this appointment, you will be provided an overview of the Phase Two Plan and its implementation, you will have an opportunity to ask questions, and we will determine if you are a good fit for the Heron Company's services.

Many thoughts and questions were zipping through Katie's mind, including analyzing the meaning behind, "determine if you are a good fit for The Heron Company's services." Even though this made her apprehensive, she was still too curious not to attend.

Ella was up now, and she headed downstairs in her pajamas. After they had breakfast, they headed off to Ella's school, Jefferson Primary, where they had a meeting with her counselor, Jamie.

Together, they decided Ella would be expected to go back to being a "normal" kid as much as possible. They agreed she was ready to start reducing the accommodations she was receiving at school, such as snacks and a break in the nurse's office during physical education. However, they also made sure that Ella understood if she needed to go to the nurse's office at any time, to just let her teachers know.

"Nobody believes I'm better," Ella told her that night. "They got used to me always sneaking snacks to them before lunch, and now they think I'm just being mean since I won't do it anymore. But they'll get over it."

Katie had to hide her laugher at her daughter's mature understanding of the situation.

"Does it feel different with things more back to normal?" Katie asked.

"Mostly it's the same." Ella played with the leftover food on her plate. "You know, except for now I don't have an excuse not to play volleyball."

"You still don't like volleyball?" Katie worried about her daughter's coordination and well-being.

"It's all right. I just don't like when the ball's coming straight at my face."

"I can talk to the school about letting you sit out."

"Nah, that's okay, Mom. It's kind of nice to be just like the other kids and have to play stuff I don't want to."

Katie enjoyed having a chance to get caught up on some projects without the overwhelming stress of Ella's illness constantly weighing on her. She hated asking her boss for more time off for her appointment at Heron Company on Wednesday, but he had been extremely supportive of Katie and seemed to understand Katie needed this meeting. So, when Wednesday came around, she dressed up a bit more than usual and headed off to it.

The Heron building was a large modern building in its own business complex, marked with a very large stone engraved with Heron's name, logo, and slogan. The parking spaces just as she entered were marked *APPLICANTS*. She figured that was her, so she parked but thought it was odd that potential new customers would be required to park so far away, especially since so many spaces closer to the building were empty. She considered moving her car, but large signs at the end of the rows warned against it.

Parking in this designated space without proper verification of your status is prohibited. Violators will be banned from the Heron Company. New plans will not be provided, and existing plans will be voided.

She decided not to risk it.

As she walked closer to the building, she saw other spaces were marked with signs indicating *PLAN HOLD-ERS* and finally, closest to the building, *PERSONS WHO ARE IN IT.*

She tried to shake off an eerie feeling as she passed through the frosted glass automatic doors into a large, open room devoid of furnishings or decoration, chilled by marble floors and walls.

Katie noticed the woman she recognized from the website walking toward her. The woman stretched out her hand to shake Katie's. On her wrist, she wore the now familiar silver Phase Two bracelet.

"Hello," she said. "You must be Ms. Sullivan. Welcome to Heron. I am Malia, Heron Induction Specialist. Follow me."

Katie followed her to a room opened by passing a key card in front of a pad by the door. Malia did not enter but gestured Katie inside. Katie found herself facing five people—three men and two women, all varying in age—sitting on the other side of a large table with a glass top and metal legs. Each was wearing that familiar bracelet, but Katie noticed one was a different color, maybe copper.

One of the male members of the panel said, "Please sit down, Ms. Sullivan. We are the Policy Compatibility Panel. We will provide you information about the Phase Two Plan, get to know you, and also work to determine if you and Heron are compatible."

Katie sat down. She wasn't exactly sure what they meant, but in spite of being nervous, she was excited to get this process started.

"We read your online submission and understand that you are looking for a policy for your daughter Ella."

"Yes, that is correct, but could you give me a little overview of your services first?"

"We offer our clients the extra time they have always wanted," he said. "Some of our clients face shorter than expected lifespans, so they are prepared to procure our services to ensure that they have ten years beyond their initial departure."

"When you say departure, what do you mean?" Katie thought she knew but wanted confirmation.

"Due to our ability to extend our clients' life experiences, we prefer to use the term 'initial departure' in lieu of death."

"Okay," Katie said, letting out a sigh she couldn't contain.

"We create a template of our policy holders. Our staff uses this template to transition a person from initial departure into their Phase Two. For a seamless transition, it is important that the template be kept up to date, and therefore, we ask clients to update their template at least every five years. If this is not kept up, the plan will be voided. Being a plan holder provides more than access to Phase Two, however. Heron Company partners, which will be outlined for you if a plan is created, provide preferred recognition to our policy holders. These partners work together with Heron to offer policy benefits relevant to their business to all Phase Two members."

"Like moving to the front of the line?" Katie asked, thinking back to her balloon-buying experience.

"Our partner companies are highly motivated to provide high-quality benefits," the man with the different-colored bracelet said. Katie could see now it was gold.

The way he made this comment made Katie feel slightly uneasy. What would make partner companies so motivated to give Phase Two members preferential treatment? There was an uncomfortable moment of silence before one of the female panel members broke it.

"If this panel finds you to be compatible with Heron, we will move forward to cover pricing and payment," she said. "You did submit your financials to Malia as described in the email?"

"Yes, of course," Katie replied.

She might have imagined it, but Katie thought the woman put a little too much stress on the word *if*. They couldn't possibly find Ella incompatible, could they? They'd as much as said some of their clients came to them because of shortened life expectancies.

What could that mean other than illness? It also bothered her that they jumped so quickly to discussing the financials.

"What makes someone compatible or not?" she asked instead, trying to bring the conversation back to a sense of normal.

"There are a variety of elements Heron considers in this process," another man said in a rehearsed vague tone. "Heron has carefully developed its process for determining compatibility and takes it very seriously," he added as if that fully answered the question.

Before Katie had a chance to ask for clarification, he began the interview process with a question of his own.

"Tell us about your job, Ms. Sullivan."

She told them about her position as administrative assistant to a mid-level executive at a construction firm.

"Describe your home to us."

Katie described the small three-bedroom, two-bathroom house she shared with Ella.

"What is your method of transportation?"

A twelve-year-old Toyota Corolla she'd bought used just before she found out she was pregnant.

After this line of questioning, which seemed highly unusual to Katie, the panel ended the interview.

"Okay, Ms. Sullivan," the guy with the gold bracelet said. "I think we have what we need."

"Is that it?" Katie said, surprised.

"The compatibility team will discuss your case and provide our decision to you within forty-eight hours."

Katie was a little on edge because she had more questions, and they didn't even ask anything about Ella, but before she could say anything, a female panel member who hadn't spoken previously stood and motioned toward the door.

"Thank you," Katie said, still confused but trying to make a good final impression.

"Malia is waiting outside and will see you out."

Stunned, Katie felt hustled out of the building but tried to stay hopeful. She thought she had done well in the interview, but it had been strange, almost completely focused on her assets and position at the firm.

She headed out to pick up Ella from school. She didn't talk to Ella about Phase Two. She didn't want to bother her with it until it was a done deal. Katie wanted Ella to just be a nine-year-old kid, and nine-year olds shouldn't have to think about that kind of stuff.

Over the next thirty-six hours, Katie could hardly sleep, and her mind continued to replay the Heron meeting. Katie checked her email often, and she always had her phone with her. She was beginning to feel obsessive.

Then it arrived.

Ms. Sullivan,

The Heron Company receives far more requests for Phase Two Plans than we can grant. Unfortunately, your compatibility score did not meet the expectations of the company.

We appreciate your interest in The Heron Company.
Sincerely,
The Compatibility Panel

Katie broke down. She didn't realize it, but this had been providing her hope, basically a guarantee that Ella could have all the time she could get. Katie felt as if she were letting Ella down, but she also felt angry. Why had she and Ella been denied? In Katie's mind, Ella was the perfect candidate, so the rejection made no sense to her whatsoever.

Chapter 5

Now that Ella was leukemia-free, Katie never again wanted to feel helpless. A Phase Two Plan would enable her to do something to help Ella if the leukemia recurred. If nothing else, Katie was practical. She wanted to have a plan in place, no matter what happened, and she was willing to do anything she could to get that plan.

Over the coming weeks, Katie spent her free time surfing the internet, trying to piece together people's experiences with the Heron Company into a more complete understanding of their practices and acceptance criteria. At first, she'd been looking for an appeals process, but her thoughts began to change.

The longer she thought back to her interview with Phase Two, the more she became convinced that compatibility for the program was determined solely by finances. The review panel hadn't asked her any important questions about Ella. All they had asked her for were her financials, her economic state, and her assets.

On a site called *The Elusive Heron,* she found others looking for answers. The site's description stated, *The*

Heron Company utilizes unjust practices to select Phase Two candidates. Help us document the practices of the Heron Company by posting your experiences here. Encourage your friends and family to do the same.

She found comments that shared similar experiences to her own. One woman said, "This felt much like a transaction with a bank." Another said, "To be told you aren't deserving of such an incredible opportunity is very hard to swallow. It really took a toll on my self-worth."

But there were others that were more positive. "Dealing with the Heron Company was such a breeze. They made me feel important." While she found both positive and negative experiences, it seemed that the majority were upset. The common thread throughout was anger.

Katie felt better after reading through *The Elusive Heron* site. She no longer felt crazy for thinking her denial was a financially based decision. Because she wanted to do something, she shared her own experience over Ella's rejection and felt slightly better.

Over the next few weeks, Katie and Ella settled into their routine. They made breakfast together each morning, usually toaster waffles covered in syrup or fresh fruit. They each had their part of the routine. Katie put the waffles in the toaster. Ella pushed down the button and grabbed the OJ from the fridge. Katie poured the orange juice while Ella grabbed the forks and napkins. After breakfast, they cleaned up and headed out to drop Ella off at Jefferson Primary. Every day Katie said, "Love you. Learn lots!"

Ella would kiss Katie on the cheek, hop out of the car, and head up the stairs to the school.

The days and weeks were passing as they continued to enjoy their new normal. After work and school, they often sat and shared the day's experiences over snacks, usually fish-shaped crackers or string cheese, two of Ella's favorites.

One day as they chatted over snacks, Katie found herself amazed by the contentment she felt with a steady routine.

"Mom, how was your day?" Ella asked.

"Good," Katie replied. "It feels nice to have a routine, don't you think?"

"Yes, it really does. I even like doing my homework."

Katie felt the grin spreading across her face. "I love you," she said. "You are such a good kid."

Ella returned her smile. "Love you, too, Mom."

After an evening of TV and dinner, Ella headed to bed. Katie was tired too but liked to enjoy a little time to herself in the evenings. She poured herself a glass of wine and sat down with her laptop to check email, get caught up on social media, and her biggest guilty pleasure, celebrity gossip. Eventually, though, she landed back on *The Elusive Heron*.

What is the point of this stupid site? she thought, upset again over her experience with Heron. *This isn't doing any good. The Heron Company is still out there, and all we are doing is bitching on some forum.*

In her anger and frustration, she clicked on the "Contact" link at the bottom of the page.

A web-based form opened, and she began to fill it out.

Name: Katie Sullivan

Comment: My name is Katie, and I am a single mom of a nine-year-old daughter. I posted my story about Heron on this site under the user name Katie_s19. Tonight I was reading the site, and I think we have to do more. This isn't enough. Heron is still out there.

Before she hit send, she second-guessed herself. *What is this person going to do? Why would they care? What am I expecting from them?* she wondered.

She hit cancel.

A week or so later, Katie received an email generated from *The Elusive Heron* site alerting her to a personal message on her public post.

Dear Katie_s19,

My name is Ian Callahan. I have been following The Heron Company for some time, reporting on their practices in The Tribune. Would you be willing to meet with me to discuss your experience with the company for an upcoming article?

Katie was intrigued but also a little skeptical and reluctant for some reason. Her recent experience with Heron, together with her need to "fix things," was causing her to want to reply. But she and Ella were happy, and she didn't want to stir things up.

Nevertheless, she couldn't combat her curiosity and asked him to phone her. She felt if she spoke with him, she might be able to leave this behind her.

She was surprised when her phone rang a little after nine. She snatched the phone up partly as a startle reflex and partly because she didn't want the sound to disturb Ella.

"Hello?"

"Katie s-nineteen? This is Ian Callahan. Is this a bad time?"

"No, not really," she responded with a hint of irritation in her tone to let him know it was kind of late. "Though my name is really Katie Sullivan."

"Nice to speak with you Ms. Sullivan. As I wrote to you, I am with *The Tribune* and have been reporting on

The Heron Company's practices. I read your post on *The Elusive Heron* site and am interested in meeting with you."

Katie surprised herself when she responded, "Shall we meet at the *Tribune* office?" There, she thought. If he were not legit, he wouldn't want to meet her at the newspaper office.

"Sounds great. How about tomorrow? Is there a time that works for you?"

"Well, my work is pretty close to there, so I could probably come down during my lunch hour. How about eleven?"

"Sounds good. When you arrive, tell the receptionist your name, and she will let me know you are here."

"Okay then. See you tomorrow, Ian."

Katie was excited about the idea of meeting with this reporter about Heron. As nice as it was to have things calm, she thought that getting out and doing something different would be good for her.

Work the next morning seemed to drag by until it was finally time to start her walk to the *Tribune* building.

She felt slightly overwhelmed by the grandeur of the newspaper's offices. A man at a large desk, in the oversized lobby, directed her to the seventeenth floor. Once there, she had no trouble locating the correct suite on her own, but she was again taken aback by the hustle and bustle of this busy space. The open area was filled with cubicles, people talking, frantically typing, and others walking briskly from place to place carrying documents.

"Hi, I'm Katie Sullivan," she told the receptionist. "Here to see Ian Callahan."

"I'll let him know you're here. You're welcome to have a seat," the receptionist said as she pointed toward a block of chairs nearby.

After just a few minutes, a man approached. He appeared to be in his late thirties or early forties. He had a full head of hair, already significantly grayed which she thought gave him a distinguished air. He wore dark slacks, shoes that appeared high-end, a light blue dress shirt and a tie, but no jacket. He also had a leather shoulder bag tossed over his shoulder and his *Tribune* badge clipped to his belt.

He walked up and slowed but did not stop as he said, "Katie Sullivan?" while extending his arm, indicating to her to get up and walk with him. "Shall we head out? There's a great coffee shop about a block away that's much nicer for lunch."

They found a table on the patio. After ordering, Ian reached into his bag to take out a notepad. He looked at Katie. "So…I read your post, and I've been working on an exposé piece about The Heron Company and its practices. I think I would like to feature you in the article."

"You would?" she asked, with a bit of hesitation and question in her tone.

She liked the idea of opening the door on Heron's practices, but she also had to think about Ella.

Ian seemed to understand she had her reservations. "Let's just start talking, and if you feel uncomfortable at any point, we can stop."

"Thanks for understanding," she said, feeling more at ease by his perceptiveness.

"To get us started, could you tell me your experience with the Heron Company up to this point?"

Katie told him about Dr. Feinberg and his Phase Two bracelet, what she had read on the internet about people's experiences with Phase Two, including people who were "in it," and about the person in the grocery store who'd moved ahead of her in line maybe just because the woman had a Phase Two bracelet. She then went into her visit to the Heron Company offices, the strange parking lot,

Malia, and her experience with the Policy Compatibility Panel, their questions, their evasive explanations, and finally, still obviously carrying a lot of emotion, her rejection.

The entire time she talked, Ian listened intently, occasionally jotting down notes.

When she finished, he said, "Wow, Katie, that is incredible. The information you gained, and your insights, have given me significant understanding. I know you must feel alone, but I must tell you that I have spoken to others who have had similar experiences. You are not the only person to suspect that they were rejected unfairly nor the only person who has noticed community favoritism to Phase Two Plan holders."

She felt relieved to know she wasn't the only one with doubts but realized she'd talked for some time.

"Shoot! It's noon. I'm going to be late."

She fumbled a bit gathering her things in her rush.

Ian stood with her. "Katie, I understand you have to go. Thank you for meeting with me. Can I please follow up with you via phone?"

Katie placed a $10 bill on the table for her coffee and scone and said "sure" as she rushed off.

Later that evening, prior to dinner, the phone rang, and Ella answered.

"Hello?"

"Hi, is your mother there?"

"Yes, who is this?"

"My name is Ian Callahan."

Ella put the phone against her belly and said, "Maaa-aaaahm iiiits eeee-aaaannn"

Katie hurried over and picked up the phone.

"Ian?"

"Katie, I just wanted to follow up with you after our conversation today."

"Ian?" Katie said. "Can I please give you a call later this evening, after, let's say, eight?"

"Sure. Let me give you my number."

Katie took down Ian's cell number and hung up the phone. When she turned around, she saw Ella looking at her.

"Who is Ian?" she asked.

Katie tried to put it off, but Ella would not be denied. "Ian works for the newspaper and wants to write about an experience I had with a certain company."

Ella looked confused and asked, "What company?"

"It's a company that offers a service I wanted, but they would not give it to me—or us."

Ella, still not totally understanding, said, "Oh! That's not nice. Sorry, Mommy."

"Thanks, Ella. Ian's trying to help others see that this company is bad, and he wants me to help him."

"Ohhhh." Ella smiled at her. "I'm glad you're one of the good guys, Mom."

Katie had been worried about how Ella would react, but it turned out okay.

When Katie called Ian later, he asked for permission to use her story in his expose of the Heron Company, and he assured her he could do so without sharing hers or Ella's real names. Katie really only thought about it for a moment before agreeing. She looked forward to seeing it in print, and Ian promised they'd talk soon.

Chapter 6

Since her conversation with her mother, Avery was more determined to find the information she wanted about the Heron Company and its Phase Two Plan. While she understood her mother's concerns that it could be some form of cult thing, she also couldn't believe a company creating a cult would advertise in such a public way. While she waited for the day of the seminar, she continued on her fact-finding mission.

Because she'd already exhausted herself trying to find information online, she decided to see if she could talk to anyone wearing a Phase Two bracelet like the woman in the commercial. She was finding the process much more difficult than she'd expected.

She spent one afternoon in the coffee shop of a busy downtown office building just to see if she could spot someone wearing the bracelet. Maybe if she offered to buy them a coffee, they'd be willing to sit down and talk with her for a few minutes. She saw one man who seemed a likely candidate. He was sitting in one of the chairs at the bar and reading on a tablet. The silver of his Phase Two bracelet winked in the sun.

Avery bought a coffee of her own then selected a chair one spot over from where the man sat, easily within talking distance without being too obvious about approaching him. She watched for a moment as he continued to read and then stopped to stare thoughtfully out the window at the passing traffic.

Gathering up her courage, Avery decided to start small. "It's a beautiful day, isn't it?"

The man offered a curt nod but nothing else. Maybe he just wasn't comfortable talking with strangers.

"I'm a college student," she told him, trying to engage him further. "I'm doing a report for one of my classes."

"Okay?" The man waited for her to continue.

"Well…" Avery started but then struggled to find the right words as she was not sure just how to approach the topic she was interested in without making the man run off. "Well, it's the bracelet you're wearing. You're a member of the Heron Company's Phase Two Plan, right?"

The minute she mentioned the bracelet, the man flipped his tablet cover closed and started putting it into his briefcase. Realizing he was on the verge of walking out on her, Avery tried a little more desperately to get something out of him.

"Please, I'm just trying to find out a little bit more about the program," she said. "I can't find out much of anything online."

"I'm sorry, miss," he responded, looking toward the exit. "I'm in a hurry to get to another appointment. Maybe some other day." With that, he took off without giving Avery a chance to say another word.

It was the same kind of experience she had with everyone else she approached. The moment she mentioned the bracelet or the Heron Company, they would suddenly clam up and find a reason to leave the room until the coffee shop baristas started giving her the evil eye.

Going home, Avery thought about the various people she'd approached and how they'd responded to her. Clearly, it had something to do with not wanting to talk about the Heron Company. Until she mentioned that, most of them had been reasonably friendly, gave no indications of being in a hurry to go anywhere, and even actually seemed interested in talking with her. Oddly, a seemingly large proportion of them had been company owners taking a mid-afternoon break. Many of them talked openly about their own companies, just not Heron.

Not knowing what else to do, Avery went home and made a list of some of the important questions rushing through her mind.

1) Why won't they talk about Heron Company? Are they afraid? Is it part of the deal?

2) Why would secrecy be part of the deal?

3) What would make company owners be afraid to talk about their plans?

4) If they're afraid, why would they still be members?

5) Not everyone is a business owner. What is different about the people who aren't business owners?

6) How can Phase Two be so popular if no one is willing to talk about it?

7) Why are people wearing these flashy bracelets and then avoiding conversation about them?

She sat and looked at her short list for a while but couldn't decide on any answers that made sense. She decided to go for a run since sometimes that helped her clear her mind and come up with solutions.

After a strenuous run around the park, she flopped

down on the grass under a tree nearest her apartment building to drink a bottle of water she'd purchased from one of the park vendors. She still had no solutions to her questions and was feeling frustrated.

"Hey, girl." Sarah's familiar voice came floating over her from behind. "Aren't you supposed to be doing research or something?"

Avery quickly spun around, surprised but pleased to hear Sarah's voice. She was happy to have someone to vent to.

"I was, but I hit a roadblock," she said.

"What kind of roadblock this time?" Sarah asked, taking a more careful approach to sitting on the grass next to Avery with an exaggerated eye roll and attitude of infinite patience.

"Well, I couldn't find anything online, so I went to the coffee shop downtown to try to talk to some people with those bracelets," Avery started to explain.

"Bracelets?"

"Yeah, you know, those silver bracelets everyone is wearing now. They look like medical ID bracelets, but they're shinier, and they say *Phase Two* on them."

"Oh yeah, I remember," Sarah said. "That company you're researching and their little secret membership code bracelets."

The way Sarah said it made Avery remember the corded friendship bracelets they used to make in their younger years. If you didn't have any, you were a nobody, and if one broke, you supposedly forever lost the friendship with the person who gave it to you.

She shared a smile with Sarah over the memory but then got back to what was on her mind. "I think this is more serious than that, though, Sarah," she said. "None of those people would talk to me. As soon as I mentioned the bracelet, they were running for the door."

"Well, you know how those super-secret groups are," Sarah said with a wave of her hand. "They all want to be part of the club, but no one wants to spill the beans that it's really all just a fancy piece of jewelry. Why are you getting all worked up about it?"

"It's not that I'm getting all worked up," Avery said. "But I have to do this report, and it seems that everywhere I turn, I'm being blocked from knowing more. Don't you think that's strange?"

"So, we're back to the cult theory then?"

Frustrated, Avery chose to look off toward the kids' climbing equipment. If she allowed Sarah to continue joking about it being a cult, Sarah might decide not to go with her to the seminar, and she might also convince Avery's mother that Avery could be getting into something dangerous.

At the same time, she needed to share her concerns with Sarah. Something she didn't want to admit even to herself was that she was becoming a little obsessive about getting to the bottom of this mystery. What was it that tied this exclusive club together?

"Most of the people I talked to today are business owners," she told Sarah. "I don't think a bunch of high-powered business people would be involved in a cult, do you?"

"Well, it isn't their standard behavior," Sarah answered. She was doing her best to look like the *esteemed* Professor Townsend from their boarding school, the one who was always going around analyzing the students' behavior and pointing out any unusual changes.

Avery giggled. "Stop that."

"So what do you think is going on?" Sarah asked.

"I don't know. I can't think of anything that would make them refuse to talk to me like that. I approached too many people for it to have been a coincidence that it was only when I brought up the bracelet or the company or the plan that they always had to run off."

"Okay, so it's definitely related to your company," Sarah said. "What else did you notice?"

"I wrote down some notes when I got home earlier. Got a minute to come up?"

Sarah grinned. "Where do you think I was heading in the first place?"

Together, they headed up to Avery's apartment, but once inside a closed space, Avery realized she needed a shower first.

"Here are all my notes so far," she said, handing Sarah a small stack of papers. "Take a look through and see if you notice anything. I'll be right back."

The top paper was Avery's list of questions from earlier in the day.

When she returned to the room, Sarah was on the couch with the TV on and a snack in hand. Avery's notes on the company were scattered across the table behind her.

"You're a lot of help." Avery cleaned off the knife Sarah had used to cut up one of the apples and pushed the core and skins down into the disposal.

"What?" Sarah said. "I didn't want to run the water while you were in the shower."

"You were supposed to be helping me find some answers about this company," Avery reminded her.

"Oh, yeah. Well, I didn't see anything all that useful. If you're supposed to write a twenty-page paper on this company, you're going to need to get a lot more information."

"Tell me something I don't know."

"Okay, smarty, did you ever think it might be part of their contract that they're not allowed to talk about the process?"

"Contract?" Avery asked.

"Yeah, like maybe they lose their plan if they talk about it."

"Why would they do that?"

"Well, you've already established it's a new science," Sarah said. "Maybe they're just trying to protect their process. Or maybe…" Sarah said, making Avery wait for it. "Maria and Duke will have the answer!" She pointed at the TV and said in a dramatic voice, "It's time for *Beachside*!"

Sure enough, Avery saw the opening title screen of Sarah's favorite show flash across the screen and knew she'd lost her friend's attention for at least the next hour. Depending on what this episode brought, she might have just lost the whole evening. Feeling frustrated, Avery gathered together her notes and decided she'd just have to wait and see what she could find out at the seminar.

Chapter 7

A month or so passed after Katie met with Ian. Somehow, sharing so many of her feelings and knowing that her story would be told gave her the mental space she wanted to enjoy her time with Ella.

She still noticed more silver and gold bracelets on the people around her. Since the incident in line for the balloon, she had other encounters when she was certain bracelet wearers were given special treatment. She didn't make a fuss over it, though. It wasn't as if she didn't notice or didn't care. She just diverted her attention to her life and to Ella.

Ella was doing well in school, and it was hard to even fathom seeing her now, compared to what she was dealing with a few months back.

After going through cancer diagnosis and treatment, she had an appreciation for school that other students didn't understand. She'd still had to go in for blood tests sometimes, but that was no big deal after the chemotherapy treatments.

One afternoon as Katie and Ella sat together at the kitchen table, Katie's phone rang "Mrs. Sullivan?" asked a male voice Katie didn't immediately recognize. "Yes. This is Ms. Sullivan."

"Hello, this is Dr. Feinberg."

"Oh…Hi, Dr. Feinberg, how are you?" Katie replied in an upbeat tone.

She remembered receiving a notice that Dr. Feinberg would be unavailable for a while due to serious health issues, but apparently, he was back at work now.

"Ms. Sullivan, I would like to meet with you and Ella. Can you come by at ten o'clock tomorrow?"

A few months ago, Katie would have been terrified by this call. She would have been nearly incapacitated by the anxiety, but she didn't have that same feeling now. She and Ella were doing fine. "Yes, we'll make it work. See you then." Katie walked back over to Ella, who was still working diligently at the kitchen table.

"Honey, we need to stop by to see Dr. Feinberg tomorrow morning, so you will have to miss the first part of school."

Ella made a face. "Ahh."

Katie knew it was because she hated missing school, even for just a half-day.

Ella finished her homework, packed up the supplies she had strewn all over the kitchen table, and helped Katie with dinner.

They were a good team. Most children hated chores, but Ella liked helping. Katie never had to ask and took a moment to appreciate that she had such a wonderful daughter. After dinner, they cleaned up and headed to bed.

The next day, they did their morning routine and headed off to meet with Dr. Feinberg.

Gail and all of the staff members in what they called, "Ella's wing," were excited to see Ella. Gail said, "Oh, sweetie, you look beautiful."

Another asked, "Girl, did you miss us here?"

As they waited for Dr. Feinberg, nurses and aides who passed by all said hi in their own way. Katie enjoyed the fact that her daughter was receiving so much positive attention and didn't stop to think what it might mean.

After a short wait, Dr. Feinberg approached looking taller and more energetic than Katie had ever seen him. As he walked closer, he made eye contact first with Katie and then Ella. "Hello, Ella, thanks for coming by. Would you mind waiting here for a few minutes? I'd like to chat with your mom first, and then we will bring you right in."

"Sure," Ella replied.

Dr. Feinberg gestured to Katie. "Follow me. We can meet in my office."

The two walked down the hall past the patient rooms. Soon the floor transitioned from tile to carpet, and the doors from white institutional paint to stained wood. They passed a few doors with placards and reached the one that read: *Dr. Laurence Feinberg.*

Dr. Feinberg opened the door to the office, which Katie knew by heart.

The walls were lined with bookshelves packed full of medical books and journals in no particular order. Piles of papers surrounded a computer on a desk set not too far from the entry. The desk and a set of chairs were out of place as a result of their cleanliness as compared to the rest of the office.

Dr. Feinberg sat down behind the desk.

"Please," he said, as he invited her to have a seat. Katie caught the flash of gold against his tanned wrist as he motioned with his arm and wondered about the "serious health issue" that had him out of the hospital for a while. As she took in these small details, Katie realized she was starting to get nervous.

"Katie," Dr. Feinberg began and then paused for a moment. "I know Ella's journey has had its ups and downs, and it has been a long road to where you two are now. Unfortunately, we have hit another bump in the road."

Katie was listening but trying desperately to make sense of what he was saying. *Bump? What could be considered a bump? Is there a problem with the insurance? Additional tests needed?*

It felt like an eternity before he continued. So many different thoughts had made their way through Katie's mind in that short period of time.

"At Ella's last follow up appointment, test results indicated that the cancer has returned."

The last four words hit Katie in the chest and threatened to shatter her. For a few moments, there was no reaction. Just complete stillness.

Dr. Feinberg continued with some words of encouragement, "The positive attitude of both you and Ella has and will continue to serve you well," he said. "I'll set up a meeting to further discuss treatment options within a few days with a new doctor."

"A new doctor?" Katie whispered.

"I'm retiring soon, and I believe you'll need to switch plans," he said. "You probably need to speak to someone in patient services."

They would have to go to a government-funded treatment plan now, Katie knew. Now that her insurance would no longer pay.

Katie was just beginning to process all that Dr. Feinberg had shared when he said, "Let's bring Ella in."

He picked up the phone to ask for Ella to be sent in.

After only a short pause, Ella walked into the office after being escorted by the front desk staff.

"Ella. Come in." Dr. Feinberg said in a welcoming

tone. "I was just telling your mother that, during your last appointment, we learned there is a reoccurrence of your cancer, and you will need to begin a new course of treatment."

In her typical way, Ella gracefully carried the burden that Katie was struggling to shoulder.

"I'll be okay. I can do it again."

This comment jolted Katie into consciousness. "Yes, Ella, we got through this. We did it before, and we will do it again."

"In the time we have now, let me know of any questions or concerns you have."

He pulled out his chair, and Katie wanted to scream. But she could barely speak. She was too much in shock.

She and Ella stood up. Katie walked in relative silence next to Ella out the automatic doors of the hospital, heading toward the parking garage. This was when Katie's motherly instincts came into play. It took her some time, but she realized that she was not supporting Ella, and she had to snap out of it. On a whim, Katie said, "Hey…Ella…do you want some ice cream?"

"Yum. That sounds perfect."

So instead of heading straight to their car, they turned and walked toward the street.

"I know there is an ice cream shop on this street," Katie told her in a much more calming and motherly tone.

"Yeah, I remember seeing it," Ella said.

"Oh, right. Yeah, there it is."

Rather than taking Ella back to school for the afternoon, mother and daughter decided to enjoy a fun day together, trying to push off thoughts of what this next round of treatments might bring. The day after they received the news that Ella's cancer had returned, Katie received a call from Ian.

"Ms. Sullivan, I know it has been longer than anticipated, but I wanted to let you know that the Phase Two piece is finally going to run in Sunday's paper."

"Oh. Okay. Thanks for letting me know." Katie was still in a fog as she responded, not only because she was still processing how to deal with her newest set of life-altering news, but also because recently, she had somehow managed to put Phase Two and Ian out of her mind.

"Katie," he asked. "Are you okay? Are you still comfortable with the piece? Remember, we are not using your real names."

"Oh, yeah, Ian. Thank you. No, it is just that Ella's leukemia has returned, and in the midst of everything, I forgot about this."

"Oh, Katie, I'm so sorry. If there is anything I can do to help you two, please, don't hesitate to let me know."

"Thank you. I will.'"

"Well, the piece runs on Sunday. I will contact you to see what you think, only if you feel up to it. If you are too busy to get back to me, I understand."

"Okay, Ian. Thank you."

"Goodnight."

Katie liked Ian. Although she had always thought journalists were pushy and would stop at nothing to get their story, he was nothing like that. He was tough. She could see that, but he didn't seem willing to put her through pain for just one more interview.

Now that she had spoken with him, and now that she was focused on everything that had happened, her anger with Heron returned.

She realized she was upset that Ella was unfairly denied a plan. She was mad that other people were getting plans and flaunting their bracelets and getting special treatment, even the doctor.

She was glad the exposé piece was coming out.

Maybe the Heron Company would get some of what Katie believed they deserved. At least, they would get a bit of bad press.

On Sunday, Ella was admitted and getting more tests, so Katie decided to wander around the hospital.

She picked up a paper at a newsstand but didn't open it. She carried it with her, under her arm, until she reached a café. She found herself an empty table, ordered herself a tea and a salad, and scanned through the paper until she found the Callahan exposé.

She started reading. He began by recounting the Heron Company television advertisements that everyone was now familiar with. He went on to give a brief overview of the Heron Company's services. There were comments from "Angela," who was actually Katie, and another person, "Rich," surely another pseudonym. Both recounted their visits and the Compatibility Panel's questions.

Some of the details were not identical, but Rich's experience seemed to have been quite similar to Katie's. There was a discussion of the bracelets that were becoming more prevalent and visible. The article made claims about their potential impact on the perceived status and preferential treatment in some settings.

Accounts of observed situations from a "Luis" and a "Brittany" that supported this claim were included.

When Katie finished the article, she took a deep breath. She was glued to the paper as she read. All in all, Katie was pleased. This should get people thinking about Heron, if they weren't already, and it would potentially confirm thoughts of others.

After Katie finished her salad, she went up to check on Ella. They wanted to keep her overnight, so Katie decided she would go home and try to get some rest.

Later that evening while at home, Katie looked for

the article online. When she found it, she started to read some of the comments, hoping to get a feel for people's reactions.

Many of the comments were in support of the article or indicated surprise.

"I was wondering what those bracelets were."

"I am so glad others have had experiences like ours."

"It is unjust to withhold these services from people who can't afford them."

Some were from those who wanted nothing more than to be heard.

"This is a cult."

"Heron is a government conspiracy."

And some spoke out against the article.

"Did these people ever consider they actually weren't compatible for some good reason?"

"Why should you get a service you can't prove you can afford to maintain?"

"Heron is a business, people, not a charity."

Katie appreciated the supportive comments and felt overwhelmed by the negative ones. Instead of feeling satisfied, she was just getting angrier.

She shut the laptop rather forcefully and set it down, flipping on the TV in hopes of calming herself down. It was starting to work.

But then a Heron commercial came on advertising a seminar to be held in the local Easton hotel downtown the following week. Katie knew she had to attend. She jotted down a note of the date and time and a website where she needed to go to register her planned attendance.

After registering, she picked up the phone and dialed Ian.

"Ian," Katie said. "There is a Heron seminar at the Easton. I am going, and I thought you might be interested."

"Katie!" He sounded a bit harsh and maybe somewhat out of breath when he answered. "It is great to hear from you. I was going to call you tomorrow to see if you picked up the paper and if you had any thoughts."

"Oh, yes. I read the piece. I thought you did a thorough job, Ian. Way to stick it to 'em!"

"I am glad you approve. As far as the seminar goes, I've already submitted paperwork to get press clearance. I am not sure how Heron is going to feel about my attendance after the piece just ran, but, hopefully, it's either already approved, or it won't get noticed among the other requests."

"Good. Maybe I will see you there."

"Yes. Katie…Take care of yourself."

"I will and thank you."

Chapter 8

Just before five on the day of the seminar, Avery went to get Sarah. Sarah was ready for dessert afterward and made it clear she was just appeasing Avery by putting up with the seminar first. When they arrived at the Easton, they noticed the vehicles in the lot were all of a nicer class than the beater of a car Avery drove. All the other cars were very new, upscale, and extremely clean.

As they crept through the parking lot, searching for a spot, the two girls realized at the same time how much her car stood out. They looked at each other briefly with both curiosity and maybe a bit of annoyance. Sarah, however, didn't seem deterred, and neither was Avery. They found a parking spot and took a closer look at what they were wearing as they climbed out of the car.

"Ummm. Do you think we're dressed okay?" Sarah asked Avery. "It seems kind of fancier than I was expecting."

"I bet it's fine," Avery said, trying to convince herself and Sarah as she said it.

Sarah looked again at their outfits and tentatively agreed, "I think we will be okay."

They headed toward the main entrance of the Easton. A doorman opened the doors for them as they approached, and Avery could see an easel with a large sky-blue sign on it just inside the double doors. The black lettering said *PHASE TWO* with an arrow pointing to the right. They followed the arrows to a room full of well-dressed people, mostly men in their fifties and some couples in the same age range. They arrived just in time as the lights flickered and the audience calmed and took their seats. A man, tall and slender in a sky-blue suit, took the stage. He was wearing a microphone headset, and a larger image of him appeared on a projection screen behind him. He was maybe forty-five years old but appeared to be wearing heavy concealer and possibly even eyeliner. Avery and Sarah turned to each other and smirked at the obvious makeup attempt.

He only paused a moment to survey the room before he started talking. "Some of you will be the lucky ones, the ones with a second chance, the ones with a backup plan. I am so glad you have decided to join us at this informational session."

The screen that previously displayed the man's image changed to display the Heron Company's name with that familiar blue-colored background. Below, it said, *The time you always wanted.* Almost unnoticed at first, the lights in the room also darkened further, allowing the screen to stand out brighter and the man on stage to fade into the shadows. Then the image faded and turned into a video. The man in the video began to tell his story. "I got married early, right out of high school, and then we had children, and I worked. I worked to support my family for forty years. I am not saying I don't love my wife or my kids, but I worked a lot, and I didn't really have time to do too much outside of that. Now with Phase Two, I am sure I will get to do all the things I dreamed of. I am sure

I will have the time I always wanted." The lights brightened slowly, and the announcer came back to the stage. "Fred, the man you just saw in the video, now has the time he always wanted. Fred had a life full of obligations that he wanted to fulfill because he is a good, caring man, husband, and father, and we here at the Heron Company believe that now he deserves his time."

Applause erupted from the audience.

"We are lucky enough to have Fred with us here tonight!" the man announced. "Fred, will you join me on stage?"

A man who appeared to be in his early seventies had been sitting in the front row. He hopped to his feet in a way that was uncommon for a man of his age and continued his enthusiasm as he jogged around to the stairs on the side of the stage. When he reached the man in the center of the stage, they shook hands, which led directly into a brief embrace accompanied by a few pats on the back, glints of silver sparking from their wrists in the stage lights.

"Fred," the announcer began, "you look like you're feeling great. What would you tell these fine people about your experience with Heron?"

"Yes, I do feel great, thank you," Fred replied. "And that is in large part due to what Heron has given me. I had such guilt for the hours I had to work and the time I missed in those years with my family, but now, thanks to Heron, I know I will have time with them. I feel alive and at peace."

"That is amazing, Fred. Thank you so much for sharing. Isn't that amazing?" he asked the audience.

The audience clapped on cue as Fred jogged offstage, back to his seat, kissing each of his family members on the cheeks along the way.

Avery wondered how having time with his family now was supposed to make up for the time he didn't have with them while they were growing up. Wasn't that the whole fun of having a family? Having time to play with your kids when they were little? She shrugged and decided that maybe it was just part of life she hadn't figured out all that well yet. She'd worry about that after college.

The lights once again dimmed and, after a short projection of the Heron Company name and slogan, another video began. This time it was a woman. She told a tale of having breast cancer and knowing her time was short. "I was diagnosed, and I fought and fought. When I was in remission, I contacted the Heron Company to get a Phase Two Plan, just in case. I was so thankful I did, because when the cancer returned, it became apparent that I wasn't going to make it. I felt comfort in knowing that because of the Heron Company, I would make it to my daughter's high school graduation." She was tearing up, even on camera, and her words were getting muddled as she fought to continue her story. "Without them, I would not have seen that beautiful moment when my daughter graduated. I am so thankful to be 'in it' and that I could be here to see my daughter off into adulthood. Thank you, Heron."

Before the lights brightened, from across the auditorium, a female voice—clearly from someone very upset—yelled, "You are saving the rich and killing the poor. My daughter deserves this as much as that woman does!"

The man came back to the stage as the lights brightened, and he did not acknowledge the woman who was suddenly being escorted out or her parting comment, "This is unjust! The Heron Company are a bunch of *murderers*!" The last part of her comments faded beyond audible range.

While the woman's outburst did spark some mild uneasiness in the audience, Avery and Sarah got the impression from the way people were looking in the woman's direction and some quiet comments around them that everyone was mostly just annoyed by the disruption, feeling the woman was rude and potentially "crazy." The people behind Avery commented they were glad that Heron had such good security to keep the audience safe. While the MC and the audience barely acknowledged the woman, Avery was intrigued.

"What was that all about?" she whispered to a wide-eyed Sarah.

"I don't know, but that woman was pissed off!"

The two redirected their attention to the stage since the presentation had continued.

The man on stage now introduced himself as Mark and moved on as if the woman hadn't existed. "As you can see from these incredible stories we've shared, we here at the Heron Company offer desirable longevity services. We provide to our account holders the promise of more time. We can offer, after initial departure from our first life, a seamless transition into Phase Two for ten additional years."

Avery leaned over to Sarah and whispered, "That's about all they'll ever say about it. When do they get to the cost? Or what they actually do?"

Mark continued, "For all interested parties, we will set up a consultation at our facility to discuss your personal situation and needs and work on setting up your Phase Two Plan."

Avery was tired and annoyed. "You mean he's not going to tell us how much this will cost? This is crap! I guess I'm going to have to set up a meeting."

"Really?" Sarah asked, her voice betraying her shock.

Avery understood this seemed like a bit too much of a step, but this was no longer just about her determination to get a good grade in her class. Now, after that woman had called out like that, Avery was even more curious about how this company did business.

She nodded, certain. "Yes, really." She gave her friend a look she knew Sarah would understand as "I need your support on this."

As everyone walked out after the seminar ended, she heard the couple behind her talking about how they were definitely going to get a plan. The seminar's vagueness and, in particular, the woman's short outburst during the seminar had Avery confused. *What was that women talking about—murderers? Why couldn't her daughter get a plan? How much are these so-called plans anyhow?*

Her head was full of questions, but she and Sarah went out to The Sweet Tooth to get dessert as promised. During the car ride, they debriefed about the seminar.

"What was Mark's deal? Did you see how well-dressed all those people were?" but mostly, "What was going on with that woman?" and "Did you see how fast they got her out of there?" Although they laughed and joked about the experience, there was an uncomfortable quality to the laughter, and Avery realized they were both more than a little disturbed by what they'd seen.

Once they arrived at The Sweet Tooth, however, their conversation diverted back to normal college stuff, and they just chatted, laughed, and had a good time. Yet Avery's mind kept drifting back to what she had witnessed. She kept seeing that woman's face and hearing her voice.

On the way home, Avery told herself tomorrow she would set up an appointment to find out more about Heron. She had two classes the next day, one at ten a.m. and one at two p.m. She could call between them.

Before class the next morning, she grabbed a paper and coffee. As she flipped through the pages, she saw an article related to the seminar. She read quickly and with excitement as it recounted the videos and the outburst from the woman. The article included a few comments from the woman, referred to as Angela (not her real name), and included a brief mention of her story. Her daughter had leukemia, and the woman had contacted the Heron Company in hopes of getting a Phase Two Plan for the child, despite monetary restrictions.

"They wouldn't return our calls, and now my daughter's cancer is back, and we have no Phase Two Plan in place," the woman said. "This company has no heart."

The article went on with short quotes from others who felt that Heron had betrayed them. Avery thought it was heartbreaking that someone's daughter had been denied a plan while in remission and remembered the woman's outburst had come just after the video of another woman who had had breast cancer. Obviously, being in remission from cancer was not enough to deny a plan. Could it be that it was all focused just on money?

Avery took note of the author of the article, Ian Callahan, and headed to class. She would contact Heron for an appointment during her lunch. When she called Heron and asked the receptionist if she could make an appointment to further discuss her Phase Two Plan setup, the receptionist asked a few questions about her age, health, marital and employment status. Once the receptionist had gotten through what seemed to be standard preliminary questions, she booked Avery for a consultation about a week later. Avery called Sarah later that day to let her know that she had made her appointment.

"Hey, I did it!" Avery said.

"Did what?"

"I booked a consult with Heron."

"Wow, crazy! Keep me posted," Sarah said.

Avery heard the note of doubt in Sarah's voice but was glad her friend had decided to just listen and support her.

Chapter 9

Thursday, the day of the seminar, arrived, and time had not at all healed the wounds from Heron's rejection for Katie, who knew the stress of Ella's relapse could have been alleviated if they had a Phase Two Plan in place. Heron Company, she felt, had cheated her daughter of her best chance. At this point, Katie was on a mission and ready to be heard.

She spent the early afternoon buying time until the seminar started since she couldn't concentrate on anything else. Another half day off work made her even more grateful for her boss's leniency and the medical leave laws. She tried to find little projects to keep her busy until it was time.

She did the dishes, she did her laundry, she checked her email, and she cleaned her bathroom, twice. Finally, at three o'clock, Katie couldn't think of anything else to keep her busy and decided it would be reasonable to start getting ready. It might be a little early, but she had to do something. She took a shower, taking extra care with her hair and makeup before trying to decide what to wear. It was hard to decide what would be appropriate. An afternoon in downtown didn't really call for all the glitz and glam she could summon out of her closet, but she remembered the impressive display at the Heron Company offices and decided she needed to dress a bit more formally than she might for work.

She decided on an outfit she felt comfortable in, even though it was perhaps a bit on the nicer side of her everyday clothes. She put on the khaki slacks and a black, loose-fitting, scoop-neck, long-sleeve shirt. She rounded out her outfit with a black pair of flat ballet-type shoes. She wasn't much of a jewelry person, but she did decide to wear her watch. It was nothing too fancy but still added a little something.

When she was finished getting ready, it was only three-forty. She'd hoped she'd managed to waste a little more time than that. The Easton was maybe thirty minutes from her house, tops, and with parking and walking in, she might want forty-five minutes total, so she had about half an hour left to kill. She could do it at home, or she could try to kill some time downtown or at the Easton itself.

She was too anxious to sit at home any longer, so she decided to just go. She knew it would be a little awkward killing time once she got there, but with all this nervous energy, she just had to move. She grabbed her purse and the keys from a basket on the ledge by her door and headed out.

When Katie arrived downtown, she decided to look for street parking, to save some money, rather than parking at the Easton's lot. She circled around the block a few times, ducking around impatient downtown drivers, gritting her teeth at the narrow streets, and trying to keep a watchful eye in every possible direction to avoid hitting any of the hundreds of pedestrians who all seemed to know exactly where they were going without any concern about their own welfare. Turning right was time consuming, due to the people crossing the walkway for the duration of the green light but turning left was out of the question. After a few trips around the block, Katie finally found a spot when a green SUV pulled away. She mentally patted herself on the back for managing to parallel park without hitting anything, despite the pressure from waiting cars and the fact that she hated parallel parking at any time, let alone with so many people watching.

Katie emerged from the parked car feeling proud of herself. She'd actually made it here in one piece, car tucked away safely in a convenient spot, and fed the meter to keep it safe for another three hours at a fraction of the cost of the Easton parking garage. She double-checked that the car was all locked up before straightening her blouse and walking purposefully toward the conference center.

She ended up taking a short cut through part of another parking lot, this one filled with nice, new cars, on her way to the main building of the hotel. As she walked, she began having a conversation with herself in her head.

"These stupid, rich people. Always getting what they want. They ride here in their fancy cars and come and pay for a Phase Two Plan. They don't care that others are being treated so poorly. How can they do this?"

Upon arriving at the main building, Katie was confronted with a set of double doors manned by a door person. Just inside, she saw a sign indicating which direction she should head.

Katie knew she was early, so she didn't expect a large crowd of people there yet. She was relieved, though, to discover she was not the first person at the seminar as several small groups of two and three people wandered around the room. It looked as if there was still some last-minute set up occurring as well.

Katie was not comfortable in these types of situations. She always felt slightly uncomfortable when she was alone. If only she could find Ian, she wouldn't feel so awkward. She headed into the auditorium nevertheless and found a seat on the right side of the room just past the center aisle and a little closer to the back than the front.

Around her, other early arrivals, sat talking with others in their group. Several couples sat, heads close, speaking quietly. Everyone around her was well-dressed, and many were in some form of business attire. She was glad she had at least picked something to wear on the nicer end of her closet, or she would have certainly felt more out of place.

She took her phone out of her purse, not because she actually needed something, but she thought it made her look less foolish if she appeared to be busy checking email or texting someone. As she flipped around from her email to the internet to different apps, she started to tune in to the different conversations occurring around her.

One pair of business-type men stood by seats over her right shoulder. They were talking about how they were ready to get their Phase Two Plan, and they sounded a bit annoyed to be at the seminar but said it "looked good."

"Hey, when is your meeting?"

"Mine is next Tuesday. You?"

"A week from Wednesday."

"I hope this doesn't take too long. I have dinner plans at Paradiseo this evening."

"I have plans too. I think it's overkill that we need to be here, but Clay said it helps with your application."

"That's why I am here, too, just to check off that little box, but I am sure my relationship with Sydney should prove beneficial."

"Connections, baby." He laughed. "Sydney said she would put in a good word for us both with the panel, but I'm here just in case."

"I will be glad when everything is signed and taken care of."

Katie closed her eyes to concentrate on what they were saying, and she didn't like any of it.

What is this? A good ol' boys' club? she asked herself.

Just then, she tuned into another couple who was sitting just a few rows in front of her, most likely a man and his wife. They seemed to be in their early seventies. Katie thought they looked cute together and wished she would one day find a relationship like that. She liked that they were older and clearly still a couple in love based on the way they were holding hands, leaning toward each other and talking earnestly while looking into each other's eyes. She could also tell the couple had money. Older people showed it in different ways than younger people did, she realized. The woman had on a pair of dark, loose-fitting slacks and a purple top that had a design worked in sequins on it. Though the top was not at all appealing to Katie, she could tell it was high quality. The man had understated clothing, but there was something about the clothes and the way he wore them that communicated they were expensive items.

The two of them were talking about friends they knew who already had Phase Two plans.

"Martin," she said, "I'm not sure about this."

"Helen, you know that Mindy and Frank have plans, and they just rave about The Heron Company. Let's just listen to the presentation. I'm sure we'll be pleased."

Katie's attention drifted away from their conversation, and she realized that now the auditorium was nearly full. There were still a few people filtering in, but the lights began to flicker to indicate it was time for the presentation to begin.

Katie sat back, her muscles tight, and thought about Ian, wondering if he had made it. She decided to try to pay extra attention just in case he didn't show up.

A man wearing a suit and a microphone headset walked out on stage. He said, "Some of you will be the lucky ones, the ones with a second chance. The ones with a backup plan."

With each word, Katie got more and more furious. Without meaning to, she sat up a little straighter and moved farther and farther to the edge of her seat.

The lucky ones! she thought. *This is outrageous.*

The seminar continued with videos of people's stories. First, a man told a tale of working hard and not having any time for himself until Heron saved the day. As if Katie was not upset enough prior to the start of the video, she became increasingly agitated as another one started of a woman talking about having had breast cancer and her gratitude to Heron for providing her the time to attend her daughter's graduation.

Unconsciously, Katie was making comments under her breath, which were likely getting louder as time progressed. Because of Heron, Ella might not even *have* a high school graduation. Without even realizing what she was doing, Katie stood up, and the fury came out.

"You're saving the rich and killing the poor! My daughter deserves this as much as that woman does!" She waved a hand forcibly in the direction of the screen.

Before she had even finished this two-sentence outburst, a team of Heron security personnel had reached Katie, each taking an arm firmly under control as they march-stepped her out. The auditorium lights began to brighten, and the man returned to the stage as if nothing had occurred, infuriating Katie even more and driving her to continue her tirade. He continued to talk as Katie yelled from just beyond the auditorium doors, "The Heron Company is evil!"

Once the doors were closed behind them, the Heron guards took Katie down the hall and into a small room that seemed set up for just such an occurrence. They pressed her fingers into an inkpad and onto a document without giving her much choice in the matter. Then another Heron employee, this one in a suit, picked up the document, passed it off to a second Heron employee who said to the guards, "Thank you. We have what we need."

The guards escorted Katie out of the building. One of them told her firmly, "This will be your last contact with The Heron Company."

The guards relaxed their grip on Katie and walked back into the building, pulling the doors closed behind them and standing just inside, daring her to try to reenter.

Katie just stood there for a few moments. First of all, she was stunned. She was surprised at herself for her outburst. She was surprised at the swift action of security and the fact that it was Heron security and not Easton security. She was also a little confused about the fingerprinting and the parting comment. Why would they even have that room ready, to begin with? Were they expecting trouble?

As she worked to compose herself, she walked to her vehicle and went over in her mind, again and again, the sequence of events that had just occurred, trying and failing to make any sense of it.

Chapter 10

Ian witnessed Katie's outburst at the seminar and was taken aback. While he knew that she was angry and felt that injustice had been done to her, he didn't realize the extent to which this had rattled her.

Ian was half-tempted to get up and run after Katie when she was escorted out, but he had to get the story he'd come after. He'd contact her later that evening and share whatever he learned.

He wanted to talk with her about any comments she had about the seminar for his piece for the following day's *Tribune,* so as soon as he finished at the seminar, he decided to give her a call.

The phone rang a few times, and Ian worried that perhaps he'd missed her, but Katie eventually picked up. To Ian, she still sounded a bit off, though her anger from earlier was apparently gone.

He wasn't sure if it was exhaustion or depression, if she had been drinking, or some combination of these, but he was immediately worried about her. It wasn't typical for him to get emotionally invested in his sources, but somehow, something about this woman and her story made her different.

It made him slightly nervous when he recognized that he was in uncharted territory with Katie, but he tried to tell himself he was drawn to her simply because of his passion for discovering the underlying truth of the story. Whatever it was, he brushed it aside as inconsequential.

"Katie," Ian said. "I was at the seminar today." He paused to leave her some room to comment on what happened there.

"Ohhh," she said, with a hint of embarrassment.

"Katie…Are you okay?"

"Ummm…I think so. This Heron Company deal is just really getting under my skin."

"Katie, I am writing a follow-up on the seminar, and it will run tomorrow in the *Tribune*. Are there any comments you would like to make for the piece?"

There was a pause.

"You know what? Okay." Katie's tone changed here. It had been low energy and apathetic, but his invitation to comment seemed to have jolted her back into the energetic and motivated woman he had begun to know. Ian recognized this and got ready to take note of what she said. "I want people to know that this company has no heart," she continued. "You can tell our story and even use our names. I am tired of hiding. Heron certainly knows who I am. They fingerprinted me when they kicked me out of that seminar and told me 'This will be your last contact with the Heron Company.'"

"What? Katie, were they threatening you?" Ian tried to pretend to himself that he was concerned for his source. Somehow, he wasn't able to quite convince a nagging voice in the back of his mind that this was all it was.

"I'm not sure."

"Will you meet me for lunch tomorrow? Not only do I want to hear more about this fingerprinting, but also I want to see how you are doing."

This last part of Ian's comment was a bit surprising to both Katie and Ian himself.

It was not as if they didn't both realize they felt comfortable around one another, but this was really the first comment that brought attention to that reality.

Katie managed to avoid making the situation uncomfortable. "That would be good. Should I meet you at your office at eleven-thirty?"

"Sounds great."

Ian was looking forward to lunch with Katie but had a lot of work to do before then. He was distracted by Katie's comment about being fingerprinted, but he had to temporarily put that out of his mind. He needed to get the piece about the seminar to press, and until he talked to Katie more, he couldn't include anything about that incident. He decided he would stick to telling Katie's story in more detail to explain her outburst to the public and sat down to write. Of course, he also summarized the seminar itself, the information provided, the video testimonials viewed, and other comments in addition to Katie's public scene, but a recap of the seminar wouldn't be complete without including something about the outburst.

Ian's article made it to press and ran the following morning and was the lead article on the paper's website. The response he received about it was mixed. Some of his colleagues were intrigued, and some stopped by to ask him for more information about Heron. He overheard others talking about the seminar and the article in general even though they didn't say anything to him directly.

However, some of Ian's colleagues were not impressed with his latest pet project. When Ian's earlier exposé on the company ran, he was warned by coworkers how dangerous it could be to home in on one topic because, for some reason or another, it hooked you. Many journalists viewed these "pet projects" with scorn and felt true journalists were those who could report on a wide variety of topics rather than pigeonholing themselves in a lost cause.

Their warnings, well-meaning and otherwise, didn't bother Ian too much. The way he saw it, it was his job to report on things people should know and, in his view, exposing information about The Heron Company was one of those things. He had a sense about this company that there was much more under the surface than he'd yet had a chance to explore. Katie's fingerprinting was just one more clue reinforcing that suspicion.

After spending the morning at the office, Ian realized Katie would be arriving any moment, so he went back to his desk, grabbed his shoulder bag, and headed toward the door. Katie had just entered and was pointing him out to the receptionist.

They exchanged hellos and, as they rode the elevator back down, they decided to head toward the Brio, the same café they went to last time. By unspoken agreement, Ian and Katie both kept the conversation limited to small talk until they were settled at their table and had placed their orders.

Finally, Ian broached the subject.

"Katie, tell me about the seminar. What got into you? What happened?"

Katie didn't look super pleased about his choice of words, but she let it go. "Honestly, Ian, I thought I was over it. Ella and I were settling into our routines and just enjoying life and one another. Then with her relapse, and the exposé, so many emotions resurfaced."

Ian was moved by her simple admission of feeling so overwhelmed with everything happening in her life. He'd been thinking of her as this incredibly strong woman to have been dealing with all of this on her own, and she was a strong woman, but even strong women could have their breaking points.

Katie continued, forcing Ian to break away from his observations. "I guess I just didn't know how to handle all the emotions, and when I got to the seminar, every word that was spoken made me more and more angry, until it just happened. It wasn't something I planned. It just came out."

Katie looked at Ian in a way that almost indicated she was looking for approval from him. She paused as she made eye contact with him, cocked her head slightly, and let out a sigh.

He had to mentally slap himself from admiring her to remember he was there in the capacity of a reporter.

"What happened when you were escorted out? You said something about being fingerprinted. Were you being serious?"

"I wouldn't make up something like that," Katie said in a stronger voice as she sat up straighter in her chair. She was relieved to switch the conversation over to Heron's behavior rather than her own. "They were in their official Heron Security outfits, not Easton. They escorted me out of the auditorium and hustled me to a room already set up just down the hall."

Ian had done a lot of research into The Heron Company, but he had yet to hear something quite like this. He nodded to indicate he was following and that Katie should continue.

"In the room, there were two people. One, a man, was sitting at a table and one, a woman, was standing near the wall. Both of them were wearing three-quarter-sleeved suits and had Heron badges. The people in the room said almost nothing the whole time I was there, which really wasn't long. The man slid a document made of cardstock toward the security guards, and there was already an inkpad on the table. Without any direction from the people in the room, one of the guards pressed my fingers into the inkpad and then onto the cardstock."

"They fingerprinted you?"

"I already told you that."

"I know," he said. "Sorry. I just can't believe they were that blatant."

"I tried not to let them, but he was so much stronger than I am, and I was in such shock. The man at the table picked up the cardstock and handed it to the woman who'd moved over to the table. She looked at the prints and then told the guards something like, 'We have everything we need.' Then the guards escorted me out the front doors of the hotel and said this would be my last contact with Heron."

"I don't know what to say."

Katie nodded. "Crazy, right!? This company is out of control."

Ian was surprised by the story and was finding it difficult to fight his rising anger at the way Katie had been treated, but it was within the scope of what he believed Heron was capable of. Still, he couldn't be just an objective reporter where this was concerned.

"What do you suppose they meant by this would be your last contact with Heron?"

"Well, I am not totally sure, but if I had to guess, I would think that they put your prints on file and will not allow you to have a Phase Two Plan."

"Do you think that is the extent of it?"

Ian wasn't so sure things were as simple as that. Neither was Katie.

"I'm not sure. Certainly, as you know, that's quite a blow, but I also have some concern that Heron has partner businesses, and that somehow I might become affected by that, but then again, who knows?"

Katie and Ian continued to hypothesize about what the guards meant exactly, and why Heron took such a seemingly innocent outburst so seriously.

Eventually, their conversation deviated from Heron, and they talked about Ella and about Ian's work, and Katie realized how much she enjoyed just talking to and learning more about him. Sooner than she would have liked, the lunch hour was over, their meals had been finished, and they both needed to return to their respective jobs.

Ian picked up the bill, claiming to Katie it was research but knowing he would never submit the expense. They gathered their belongings and headed out for their short walk back.

Ian felt sorry for Katie and maybe even a little motivated by her incident with Heron. After learning more of her story with Ella, realizing she had never had help raising such a sweet child, Ian thought Katie had already dealt with so much heartache and disappointment in her life. He was sad to see her dealing with something else, and he was also worried, knowing Heron was already a very powerful company, judging by the clientele he'd managed to track thus far. He was concerned that being on their bad side, which from the sound of it Katie most certainly was, could bring her even more trouble.

Before they each headed off in different directions, Ian promised Katie that he would investigate the fingerprinting incident to see if anyone had experienced anything similar. He also promised to keep in touch, for research purposes of course.

Chapter 11

Avery's appointment at Heron to discuss a Phase Two Plan for herself was set for one week after the seminar.

"I haven't been able to find out anything substantial about Heron so far. I wonder if this appointment will finally give me the answers I need for my paper," she was telling Sarah during a shared lunch.

Sarah rolled her eyes.

"What?" Avery managed to sound offended and innocent all at once.

"That's all you've been talking about for the past four days!" Sarah didn't hide any of the exasperation from her voice. "I can't wait for you to get this meeting over with so we can stop talking about it already."

"I can't help it if I'm nervous about this paper."

"Is that really all you want out of this?"

Avery bit her lip. From what she'd seen of Heron Company, getting accepted for a Phase Two Plan was a clear sign of belonging to a so-called better class of people. While Avery had attended prep boarding school, she had been among the poorer of the upper middle-class kids who attended. There was a part of her that just wanted to belong.

"I'm not sure what I want, other than some answers," she finally told Sarah. "I want to know more about what they do and, after that woman's outburst at the seminar, I'm even more interested in knowing about their practices and intentions. How do they screen people for their service anyway?"

"Just be careful," Sarah said. "Don't get sucked into their sales hype."

Avery scoffed. "You know me better than that. I've always tried to question the companies I choose to do business with."

Sarah nodded in agreement, and Avery chose to ignore the hint of doubt that still hung around her friend.

When the day arrived for her appointment, Avery was feeling anxious. She didn't usually get flustered easily and wondered what this nervousness was really all about.

Despite setting her alarm early, by the time she rolled out of bed, took her shower, got dressed, had some coffee, and was ready to leave, she was already a few minutes behind the schedule she set for herself. She grabbed her bag and keys as she headed out the door.

She drove a little bit faster than usual and balanced that with following the navigation to Heron. When she arrived, she pulled into the Heron complex parking lot and parked in the first spot she saw. This was fairly typical for Avery. She wasn't one to waste time circling a lot for a prime spot. This was especially the case today, because, while she wasn't late, she was not arriving at a time that allowed her to be leisurely.

Once she had parked the car and climbed out, she noted signage indicated parking space designation. She read the sign near her spot with a brief moment of panic and annoyance that she might need to move her car when she was already behind schedule. The sign said *APPLI-CANT*, and while she wasn't certain this was her, she was pretty sure it was so she headed off toward the building without a second thought about it. As she continued toward the building, though, she noticed the other strict warnings about parking in the lot, which only added to her sense of anxiety about the importance of this meeting.

When she approached the main entrance, two large doors of frosted glass slid automatically open, and she found herself in a large lobby. Once inside, she was greeted by the woman from the website who now introduced herself as Malia.

"Avery, I'm glad you arrived on time," Malia said with a pointed glance at her wristwatch. "Your appointment is scheduled to begin shortly, so I suggest we head there immediately."

"Sounds good to me." Avery was surprised Malia knew who she was but realized she was probably the only appointment scheduled at this time. She hurried to catch up to her.

At a brisk pace, Malia's high heels clicked on the tile floors, as they climbed up a flight of stairs, and tapped down a hallway to an unassuming door.

"Your panel will be right inside. Are you ready?"

Avery thought so, but now that Malia asked the question in that way, she wasn't so sure. She had no idea what this panel was all about and what she needed to be ready for.

Despite this, she said, "Yes, I am. Thank you."

Malia gave Avery a smile, passed a keycard over a panel near the door, and indicated to Avery that she should enter, which she did.

Avery discovered a fairly empty room on the other side of the doorway and a somewhat creepy panel of

Heron employees seated at a table. The Heron employees were all wearing uniforms. She noted that they all had Phase Two bracelets that were very visible, due in part to the fact that the uniforms were three-quarter sleeved. Avery noticed this unusual uniform styling right away and felt certain it was done on purpose to make the bracelets more visible.

"Please have a seat."

Before Avery had much time at all to get settled into her seat, the questions began.

"What is your occupation?"

"Student," she responded.

"What is your major?"

"Undecided."

"Do you have any affiliations inside or outside of school that are noteworthy?"

"I'm not sure. I was a member of Key Club at my last school before college."

"What are things you think helps a person be successful?"

"Hard work, I guess. A positive attitude."

While Avery was unclear about why the questions were being asked at what she believed was a medical screening, she continued to answer as the questions came at her rather quickly, one after another.

The only woman on the panel—a woman dressed in a white smock—asked, "Would you tell us about your trust fund? When will you gain access to it?"

Avery was taken aback.

"I'll need to check the paperwork," she managed to reply.

She knew she had completed financial paperwork for the meeting, but the panel seemed a bit too well versed in her situation, given how recently she had submitted the information.

"Of course," the woman said and smiled back at her. "Can you tell us why you want this?"

Even though Avery was skeptical about the questions asked, she was usually very good with people. Almost everyone she met remembered her and liked her so she turned on the charm and waited for her chance.

"Who wouldn't?" she said.

The panel members laughed, and finally, they gave Avery a chance to ask some questions of her own.

She decided to start with the most burning question in her mind—how much did a service like this usually cost?

Prior to answering, the panel exchanged glances, and the woman said, "Pricing is something that we will discuss at an upcoming meeting. Please indicate to Malia on your way out that you need to schedule Appointment B. We will change your status in our system to indicate that the panel has deemed this appropriate. Congratulations."

Avery headed toward the door to meet Malia, confused. The man on the panel had congratulated her, but she wasn't sure what had happened.

When she reached Malia, she didn't have to tell her that she needed another appointment. Malia was standing poised and ready. She got straight to the point as Avery approached. "I see your status has been updated, and I have scheduled you an appointment next week at the same time. Congratulations."

Another congratulations? Interesting. Avery found herself feeling a little proud because of these kudos, even though she still wasn't sure exactly why.

Malia escorted her to the doors without any further comment, walking fast enough that Avery almost had to run to keep up. As the front doors opened, Malia again said that they would see her next week and ushered Avery out.

Avery headed back through the parking lot and to her car, still wondering just what had happened. Had she just been approved for a plan? Did she even want one? What had she managed to find out?

She called Sarah as she drove back. She really wanted to tell someone about the experience, but Sarah didn't answer. She left a longer than appropriate message recounting the visit to Heron and said they should get together soon.

When Avery arrived back home, she sat down trying to process her visit to Heron.

Strangely, even though she felt the process showed some elitist tendencies, that she acknowledged and that concerned her, she also felt pleased to have a second appointment and she was intrigued about what it had in store.

Eventually, she opened her laptop and went back to the site where she first found stories about Phase Two and Heron.

Impulsively, she started typing her story onto the site, *The Elusive Heron*, under the moniker AJ. She felt she just needed to talk with someone about what happened to see if they could help her find more meaning in the event. When it came down to it, she had a pretty interesting day and just wanted to talk about it with anyone.

One week later, Avery still wasn't sure what to expect regarding her second appointment with Heron, but she did know she wanted to be on time. Without thinking much about it, she dressed up a bit more than for her last appointment, even taking the time to select the outfit the evening before. She chose black slim-legged jeans, a shirt, and a business casual style blazer. It wasn't anything fancy but was more refined than Avery's daily wear.

When she arrived at the Heron complex for the second time, she felt a little more comfortable. She still parked in the first spot she found, but this time she was confident that it was an acceptable *APPLICANT* spot, and she no longer felt quite so intimidated by the signs. She headed toward the large frosted green glass doors at the entry and was prepared when they opened, and Malia was standing just inside.

"Hello, Avery," Malia said. "Please follow me."

Malia walked with the same poise, and the same click of her high heels could be heard as she led Avery to her appointment.

Malia walked Avery upstairs again. A man approached them at the top of the stairs. He was tall with an athletic build and a dark complexion. Malia introduced Avery to him.

"Avery, this is Tyson. He will take you through your second appointment."

"Nice to meet you," Avery said, and they shook hands.

Malia headed back to the lobby, and Avery walked with Tyson.

"Today I will take you around the Heron complex, and we will discuss additional steps. How does that sound?"

"Sounds good," Avery said, mostly because she wasn't sure what else to say.

"So, I assume the compatibility panel outlined the general process?"

"Um, not exactly," Avery said, remembering how confused she'd been following her last appointment. All they'd seemed to talk about was her future potential and her financial information. She still didn't feel she knew anything about how the Phase Two Plan was supposed to work.

"Walk with me, and I'll explain," Tyson said.

Uncertain as she was, Avery followed along.

"Basically, you are given a ten-year life extension after your initial departure—we here at Heron prefer to use the term 'initial departure' in lieu of death—using a template that we create for you and which you will need to update at least once every five years to keep it current."

"I don't really understand that," Avery interrupted. "What is a template exactly?"

Tyson chuckled in a friendly way. "You'll see soon enough. Now, about the updates. You are encouraged to update as often as you'd like. Keep in mind that, in the event of a sudden departure, your template will only be as current as your last update. So don't go getting married or something and forget to update, or your husband might get a nasty surprise when you come home and don't remember who he is."

"So that template," she asked, feeling numb. "It will help me live ten years longer?"

"Yes, exactly," he told her. "After that, you'll have another bracelet upon your return." He lifted his sleeve and tapped his own. "Gold," he said.

As they walked the halls, Avery found she got along well with Tyson. She felt at ease around most people, and, as a result, others relaxed around her.

"As you can see, the facility has significant security features, and we take the protection of our clients' policies very seriously," he continued, pointing out the security panels located at each door.

"Certainly. I can see that."

"In this wing, we file client templates."

"Oh...so that's why there are so many security guards."

"You've got it."

The company's extreme precautions now began to make much more sense to Avery.

"We're heading past a wing where clients who have initially departed are admitted, Phase Two is initiated, and they are eventually discharged to resume their lives. Due to the nature of the procedures carried out, we will not be touring that part of the facility."

"Top secret, eh?" Avery attempted to joke, but her laughter caught in her throat.

Tyson replied, "Yes, ma'am," with a little too much seriousness.

In spite of her joke, Avery was curious about that part of the facility. Were there dead people in there? How did one enter Phase Two?

"These are our Heron offices," Tyler said. "Here people work on advertising, marketing, seminars, and the day-to-day running of the company."

Avery noticed that this area was significantly busier than the others. Most of the Heron facility was fairly empty with a few nicely dressed workers here and there and Heron Security stationed at regular intervals, but this area was much like a regular office building. Avery wondered how you reached this area from the parking lot. She didn't see workers entering anywhere when she arrived, and it wasn't visible from the parking area.

Tyson and Avery continued to walk, and, finally, they entered a room with a table. After they sat down, Tyson began to outline future steps to Avery. He flipped through a document as he spoke.

"I will write and submit a report outlining our appointment. We have your financials in our system from your compatibility meeting, so all we need now is authorization to proceed."

Avery looked over the document that Tyson had been referring to. She initialed that she attended the compatibility panel appointment and had been given a tour of the facility. She also initialed that an outline of the Phase Two procedures had been provided to her. She wasn't totally sure on this one, but then she thought: First, template; second, initial departure; third, admission to Heron; fourth, Phase Two initiation; fifth, depart in it; *and then I will have ten years beyond my initial departure date.* Now it all seemed so simple and straightforward.

She read the financials section as best she could. It required what Avery felt was an exorbitant deposit to become an initial Phase Two policy holder, and on top of that, a hefty per year fee just for "maintaining the policy." For the first time, she actually felt a little grateful to Reuben for giving her the trust fund that would make this possible. Though she didn't have access to it quite yet, the paperwork clearly referenced the fund as a payment source. Before she knew it, she had signed the financials section.

She turned to Tyson and half-jokingly said, "So when do I get my bracelet?"

He smiled. "At your next appointment. Once your template is on file, you will be provided a Phase Two bracelet to indicate your policy, both to hospitals, so they understand to bring you here upon departure, and also for our partner organizations to recognize you as a policy holder."

Chapter 12

It had been a few weeks since she and Ian last spoke, and Katie was starting to feel impatient again. Ella's treatments had to be aggressive to combat the cancer that was seeping back into her system, so she was spending much of her time in the hospital, leaving Katie with too much time to think. With every treatment session, Katie was reminded again that her daughter had been denied the security of a healthy life, even if for only ten years, by a company she was more and more convinced was motivated by greed and power.

Ella's new doctor, Dr. Nichols, was a nice young man with a friendly disposition, although he often looked tired. He also didn't wear a Phase Two bracelet, which made Katie feel a little better. The process of adjusting to the new doctor and insurance could be trying at times, so his cheerful approach certainly helped.

Katie felt it was nearly impossible to reach Dr. Nichols for questions and debriefing. His assistant, Tina, was the one who often provided her information and updates. During one of their conversations that week, Tina asked,

"Dr. Feinberg did tell you Ella's particular form of leukemia is more aggressive than others, correct?"

"Yes," Katie answered, wishing her insurance had allowed them to stay with Dr. Feinberg until he retired so she wouldn't have to keep going over the same old information.

"I know it is frustrating to have to be going through this all again after believing you were so close to cured," Tina said, acknowledging Katie's frustration, "but I need to make sure you understand everything."

Dr. Nichols was one of a small network of doctors who accepted the government's supplemental insurance such as Katie's. Situations and frustrations such as these were obviously not all that unfamiliar to Tina. Katie recognized some of the techniques she was using as standard techniques for diffusing escalating emotions.

"Dr. Feinberg was pretty thorough," Katie said. After the words were out of her mouth, she realized they might have sounded critical of the younger doctor.

"I am sure he was," Tina said. "It may take some adjustment as you transition to Dr. Nichols's care." Tina continued, trying to educate Katie a bit on the ins and outs of the complex world of health care and insurance. "Dr. Nichols is a very hard-working man and has dedicated his life to helping individuals with situations like yours."

Katie understood that transitions took time, but she wondered what Tina meant by *situations*. "What do you mean?" she asked.

"Well, while Dr. Nichols and Dr. Feinberg are in the same building, Dr. Nichols was recommended to you because he accepts your insurance. Dr. Feinberg and many other physicians choose to work exclusively with privately insured patients."

This reminded Katie. "Actually, where is Dr. Feinberg?" she asked as she hadn't seen or heard from him since he introduced her to Dr. Nichols. "I would have thought he'd have some interest in how his former patients were doing."

"You didn't know?" Tina asked. "After Dr. Feinberg suffered a massive heart attack some time ago, he decided it was time to retire. He only came back to close out his records and finish up with a few patients. He's down in Florida now."

"Oh, wow!" Katie said. She'd been aware of a health issue and that he was considering retirement, but she had no idea it was a serious heart attack. "I'm glad he was able to survive the heart attack and enjoy some retirement." As Katie finished her sentence, she remembered the changed color of Dr. Feinstein's Phase Two bracelet and suddenly realized why he'd looked so healthy the last time she'd seen him. He'd started his Phase Two Plan and was now enjoying the extra ten years of life Ella had been denied.

She barely heard the next words from Tina and had to struggle to pay attention as she continued with the original purpose of her conversation with Katie and provided her with Ella's prognosis.

"If she comes through these treatments all right, it will be important to keep her a bit more isolated for a while because of the risk of outside infection," she was saying. "Her immune system will be especially weak."

"When will she be able to come home?"

"There will be one more week of intensive chemotherapy, and Dr. Nichols will keep her here for observation. If she handles that all right, she can come home after that, but she will not be able to attend school yet as the threat of infection is too high."

Katie finished up with Tina and hurried back to work still fuming internally at the Heron Company's lack of compassion.

With thoughts of Ella's weakness dominating much of her attention, Katie spent much of the following week going back and forth between work, the hospital to visit with Ella, and home trying to sterilize everything to keep her daughter safe. Her anger at Heron Company always burning just beneath the surface, she felt like a time bomb getting ready to explode by the time Ian called to check on her.

"I wanted to find out how things are going," he said, his soft voice came through the phone line the night before Ella was scheduled to come home.

"I'm going crazy," Katie admitted, too tired to care what kind of impression she made. "Ella's coming home tomorrow, I still need to wash all the sheets and spray the counters. I wanted to get to the grocery store for some of her favorite treats, and I just had another incident where I had to wait as one of these stupid bracelet-wearers got to go ahead of me in line, and Ella won't be able to go to school, so I need to take time off from work again and she—"

"Whoa!" Ian interrupted. "Slow down." The concern in his voice was clear even in Katie's frazzled state. "How can I help?"

"You can't." Katie wanted to cry with frustration. "Not unless you know a good cleaning lady who can come over at the last minute."

"As a matter of fact, I do," he said. "Tell me your address."

"Ian, I can't afford any help. Didn't you hear me? I need to take more time off work, and I don't have any more sick or vacation days. This is all going to be unpaid."

"Don't worry about that. This particular cleaning person just wants to help."

It was completely out of character for her, but Katie was feeling overwhelmed with everything at that moment and wanted nothing more than a friendly voice to get lost in for a while. Uncharacteristically, she gave Ian her address and was somewhat pleased to see him pulling into her driveway twenty minutes later.

For the next hour, Ian helped Katie get the house cleaned the way she wanted it to be with Ella coming home, then the two headed to the grocery story to stock up on items for Ella. Katie was actually starting to feel better and more refreshed when another bracelet incident, as she was starting to call them, occurred at the checkout counter.

All the lines at the grocery store were quite long, and Katie and Ian made their way to one that appeared to have just opened as it had almost no line at all.

"I'm sorry, sir, this line is reserved for our premium customers only," the clerk said as if he said this sentence hundreds of times a day.

"What do you mean 'premium customers'?" Ian demanded.

"That's all I can say, sir."

"How do you know I'm not a premium customer?"

"I can clearly tell," the clerk answered blandly, motioning toward Ian's wrist.

Ian was now pretty wound up himself. "Let me get this straight," he said. "Even though you have no one in line here and are perfectly capable of ringing us up right now, we have to go over there and get in one of those lines?" Ian pointed to the long lines behind him.

"I'm sorry, sir, this line is reserved for our premium customers," the clerk said, repeating himself verbatim from his first comment.

"Is there a manager around?"

Katie was also upset by the situation, but she had never considered actually pursuing it to the manager level and was fascinated to watch as Ian's journalist skills pulled out a new story for his paper from the store manager. Ian and Kate talked more about what they had been learning about Phase Two, the Heron Company, and the power it seemed to be gaining as they made their way back to Katie's house.

"It's a slippery slope when companies start making policies like this," Ian said to Katie as they pulled into her driveway. "I'm worried about where it's leading."

"I hear you," Katie said.

"I know it's getting late, but let's check *The Elusive Heron* site," Ian suggested once they'd finished unloading the car and putting the groceries away. "We should at least get this conversation started."

"What's that?" Katie said when the site finished loading.

It was a new message posted by someone identified as AJ who had apparently had a positive experience with the company and went into more detail than usual regarding her experience.

...the compatibility panel meeting was surprisingly short, and they said that on the way out I should schedule appointment B. Everyone congratulated me as I exited. I am a bit in awe, because I was expecting something much more difficult. Just had to share with someone. AJ

"That's different," Ian said after they both read through. "Most of the time they just end with 'someone will contact you within 48 hours.' I've never heard of anyone being offered a second appointment on the spot like that."

"This AJ seems more willing than others to share, too. Look how much detail they put into their description," Katie added.

"If you don't mind, I'd like to contact this person. Maybe they can give us more insight into what happens behind the closed doors."

"Be my guest," Katie said with a wave at her laptop keyboard.

Ian drafted a "personal message" directly through *The Elusive Heron* site.

AJ,

My name is Ian Callahan, and I am a reporter for the Tribune. I just read your post recounting your experience on your first appointment with Heron.

You indicated in your post that you felt your panel meeting was "surprisingly short" and that at the conclusion of the meeting you were instructed to schedule a B appointment.

I have been investigating The Heron Company for some time now, and I have yet to come across someone who had an experience such as yours. In particular, I have not heard of or met any individual who has been granted a B appointment at the time of their initial appointment.

As you can imagine, I would very much like to sit down with you and talk further. If you are so inclined, please contact me either by phone or by email.

Thank you,
Ian Callahan

Ian provided both his email and his phone number at the end.

"I hope they'll get in touch with you," Katie said.

"Me too," Ian agreed. "Now, would you like to enter our experience from today into the site, or shall I?"

Together they drafted a short message about their experience and asked if anyone else had similar restrictions. Katie was nervous about sharing the experience, knowing the manager would remember them, and was concerned about what that might mean in the future, but then she remembered Heron had already fingerprinted her and was apparently keeping her information on file somewhere. That gave her the spark of anger she needed to go ahead and press the send button.

By then it was getting rather late, and Katie wanted to be at the hospital early the next morning.

"I guess I should get going," Ian said. He seemed reluctant to leave.

"Yes, well, I do have to get up early," Katie admitted.

"So, I hope Ella enjoys all her treats."

"Oh, I'm sure she will. Thank you so much for your help. I don't know how I would have gotten it all done without it."

"Call on me anytime," Ian said, looking at Katie longer than was probably appropriate. Katie didn't really notice as she was looking back at him.

"Well, goodbye," Ian said with a little shrug.

"Goodbye," Katie said, walking him to the door and holding it open as he made his way to the car. As his car pulled away, Katie wondered what it might be like to have a life that allowed her time for friends like him.

She shrugged as she closed the door. Ella would be home tomorrow, and having her daughter was enough.

Chapter 13

"Avery, I'm worried about this whole Heron Company thing," Sarah said the moment Avery answered the phone.

"Come on, Sarah, not this again. You were there at the seminar."

"I know," Sarah said. "But I still worry since you are getting so involved, with going to the appointments and all."

"I get it, but I have this paper deadline," Avery said, feeling like she had to justify herself. She had been excited to tell Sarah about her experience at Heron, but now she wasn't so sure. Her friend didn't seem interested in sharing her enthusiasm.

"You just seem so wrapped up in this thing," Sarah pressed. "Is this really about the paper anymore?"

Avery honestly hadn't thought much about it prior to this question. She paused for a moment. "I guess not entirely. Yes, I have to finish this paper soon, but honestly, I guess it is more than that now. It feels like something weird is going on here."

With this burst of honesty from Avery, Sarah backed

down. "Okay, well hopefully at least with all this effort, you will get a stellar grade on that paper."

Avery giggled, wrapped up their conversation, and the two hung up.

Reminded she had a paper to work on, Avery spent the next few hours jotting down some notes toward her project.

She was heading out to the gym when she thought to check for any important messages. The voicemail icon was active, so she started the message.

"Hi, Avery, it's Mom. I was just checking in. Marshall and I are back from our vacation, and I remembered you were going to some seminar or something, so I wanted to hear how that went. Give me a call when you have a chance. Love you."

Avery decided she would call back later. Realizing she hadn't talked to her mom in a while, Avery felt like they should touch base. But her nerves were raw again, remembering the insinuation in her mother's voice when they discussed the seminar before, and she wasn't quite ready to deal with that yet.

She decided she should also probably check her email too but wanted to get going so just checked it with her phone. She had eight new messages. Junk, Junk, Junk, email from Sarah. The two girls rarely found themselves irritated with the other, so Avery was relieved that Sarah had already written to apologize.

Avery,

I was surprised when I found these and thought you might find them interesting. They might help with your report.

The first link took her to a fairly lengthy *Tribune* article. She noticed the writer's name was Ian Callahan and although she wasn't certain she was pretty sure that was the writer who wrote about the outburst at the seminar. She could see the article was older than the one she remembered reading about the seminar, and it recounted some people's visits and experience with the Heron compatibility panel.

She skimmed through farther, and a few lines jumped out at her.

Heron's practices in policy allocation are unfair.
Family is denied policy and deemed incompatible, but no reasons were provided.
Heron denies child in remission a policy.

Avery wanted to read in more detail, but it would have to wait because she was at her car. She made a mental note to read the article more carefully later that night. For now, she just wanted to lose herself in some strenuous physical activity for a while. She needed some time to process.

Heading through the big double doors leading into the slightly bleach-tinged entry foyer of the gym, Avery noticed the time on the giant clock that hung above the main counter. She stepped briskly up to the counter to swipe her card just moments before another woman approached.

"Just made it on time for the five-thirty aerobics," she said with a smile to the woman behind the desk and reached to grab the sign-in ledger.

The woman stopped her from pulling it all the way to her, but Avery could see at a glance that all the sign-in spots had been filled already. "I'm sorry, that class is already full," the woman told her. "The equipment room still has some available machines, though."

"Oh, well," Avery tried not to look dejected. "I guess

I'll just do the elliptical or run on the treadmill, then."

She scanned her card. As she walked away from the counter, she heard the woman behind the desk tell the other woman. "Enjoy the class."

There was only one class being offered at five-thirty, an aerobics one that was already full. Since the gym didn't take reservations, all classes were first come, first served. Avery couldn't help turning her head to take a look at what was going on.

Standing there at the desk was a lovely blonde woman in her early forties who was wearing an expensive-looking coordinated workout outfit. Even her shoes were well kept and clearly used only for indoor workouts.

Then Avery saw it. The woman was wearing a Phase Two bracelet.

As she continued toward the locker rooms, Avery found herself becoming angry and jealous that the other woman had been able to take the spot she should have had.

That's not fair, she thought. *I was here first.* Her next thought was, *I wish I already had my bracelet, so I could be going to aerobics.* But then she started questioning what she perceived to have occurred.

Did the woman really arrive after her? Could she have come earlier and signed up and then returned? Could she have just run to her car or something? She had already been in her workout clothes. Maybe Avery was making more of this just because of the article Sarah sent.

Avery thought about this for the first part of her workout, but her mind eventually wandered to other things. Once she felt like she got in a good workout, she headed home. She knew she wanted to finish reading that email from Sarah, and if there was time, call her mom.

After getting home, showering, and getting into some comfortable evening wear—in Avery's case, yoga pants and a tank top rather than official pajamas—she poured herself a glass of water, took down a box of crackers from the cupboard, grabbed her computer, and flipped open her email. She still had a few unread messages to sort through before she felt she'd be able to focus on the links from Sarah.

Gym newsletter, email reminder about an upcoming appointment, and an email from *The Elusive Heron.*

AJ,
You have received a personal message through The Elusive Heron. To view the message, click here.

Avery clicked.

She found a message signed by a Mr. Ian Callahan. He introduced himself as a reporter, claimed that her experience with Heron was not typical, and said he wanted to talk with her about it.

This is odd, she thought. *Wasn't that link from Sarah to an article by this fellow?*

She clicked back to Sarah's email.

Indeed, it was.

Avery carefully read each link sent by Sarah, and she certainly was getting alarmed by what she read.

She did not like the idea of doing business with a company with questionable practices and remembered what it felt like at the gym. On the other hand, part of her really wanted that Phase Two Plan and that bracelet.

She decided to give Sarah a call.

"Hey, Sarah. It's Avery."

"Oh, hey. How are you?"

Avery could hear the note of hesitation in her friend's voice and decided to call a truce immediately. "Good. I got those links you sent. Crazy! I am not sure what to make of it."

"I thought you might find them interesting. I'm not sure you should be giving this company your business."

"Well, you want to know what is really weird?"

"What?"

"The other day I posted on *The Elusive Heron* just because I wanted to talk to someone about it, and no one was around. The guy who wrote one of those articles you sent me, Ian Callahan, sent me a personal message regarding my post."

"What? Why?"

"He said it was unusual for them to give someone a second appointment without a waiting period, and it sounded like he wanted to hear more about it."

"Well, are you going to meet with him?"

"I'm not sure. He's a reporter, so I'm not sure of his motives. What do you think?"

"I don't know, but if you want backup, just give me a call."

"Thanks," Avery was relieved to know Sarah was supporting her. She hated it when there was any kind of tension between them.

"Either way, keep me posted. This is kinda crazy."

"Right?"

"Totally! Take care. Talk to you soon."

"Okay. Bye."

"Bye."

Avery sat there trying to decide how she felt.

Even more than ever, she wondered about The Heron Company's practices. It seemed like Ian Callahan might just be the person who could help her and give her valuable insights. By now, it was more than just information for a report she wanted. She needed to know what going on.

She also wondered if there was something to what Ian Callahan was saying. Was she treated differently for some reason? If so, she certainly wanted to know why.

Well, that was it. She was going to meet with Ian. She began to draft a reply to Mr. Callahan. She wondered if she should mention her paper in her response, but she worried that he might be reluctant to meet with a college student, and even though he was the one to request the meeting, she was actually starting to get her hopes up about the information he might be able to provide her and didn't want to risk losing that opportunity.

Ian,

I received your message, and I am willing to meet with you. There are some things about The Heron Company that make me curious. My concerns have been heightened after reading through your message, a couple of the articles you have written, and my experience at a seminar in which a woman yelled out about her frustrations. Now that I know a little about her through your stories, I want to know more.

Please reply and let me know when you would like to meet. I am available most days after 5.

Thank you,

Avery Jensen (AJ)

For the next couple of days, Avery went about her business in something of a daze. She had a lot on her mind. Then it came. She checked her email as she usually did in the morning, and there was a message from Ian.

Avery,

Thank you for responding to my email. I am looking forward to meeting and talking with you. I can meet with you any evening this week. You can come to my office. The Tribune office is downtown in the Wencler building. I am going to suggest Tuesday at 6 P.M. Let me know if that

*will work for you or if you have a different time that
would be preferable.*

Thank you and looking forward to our meeting.
Ian

Avery liked that Ian had suggested they meet at his office. Getting downtown was not the most convenient thing for her, and parking there was a bit of a challenge, but she felt safer about meeting at the newspaper, and by six o'clock, most of the office workers would be gone, which should make parking possible. She would have to skip her workout that day to make the meeting which she didn't like to do, but she decided it was worth it. She wanted to know what was going on with this company. Especially before she got further involved with them.

She sent Ian an email to confirm the meeting.

Ian,

Tuesday at 6 will work just fine. I will meet you at your office.

See you then,
Avery

Avery was surprising herself a little. She was someone who trusted people maybe more than other people did, and she certainly got along well with almost anyone, but this meeting was even beyond what Avery knew herself to be comfortable with. For some reason though, she was excited and anxious to meet with Ian.

She did not like the idea at all of a corrupt company out there playing God. If that really was the case, she knew she would want to do something about it. She was hoping it wasn't the case that this company had inappropriate intentions, but ignorance was not bliss to her. She wanted to know whom she was dealing with.

On Tuesday, Avery decided that she would study until five-fifteen and then head downtown. Of course, when quarter after came, it caught her off guard. She had been looking around on the internet and when she glanced at the time on the upper right corner of the computer screen it was already five-eighteen.

Shoot! she thought to herself. She was going to be late.

Well, that was typical.

While she was waiting for the computer log out to complete, she tossed her items into her bag. Once the computer shut down, she grabbed her coat and hurried out the door with her phone in hand. She glanced at the screen without missing a beat. It was five twenty-three. She walked toward her car as she typed "Wencler Building" into her phone's GPS. She was pretty sure she knew how to get there, but she figured she'd better play it on the safe side.

Despite the traffic, she had the Wencler Building in view at five fifty-three. But that wasn't going to get her to her meeting on time. Once she found a parking spot, grabbed her bag, locked up, and headed toward the building itself, it was five fifty-nine.

"Okay, this isn't so bad. I'll be in the office by six-ten. That's reasonable," she told herself.

After checking the building's directory to find that the *Tribune* offices were on the seventeenth floor, Avery hopped on the first elevator she saw. As soon as the doors closed, she knew she had made a mistake. This elevator only served floors two through nine. Now it was six-oh-six.

Great! she thought.

Luckily there were only a few people on the elevator, but she would have to go back to the lobby. She reached it at six-oh-eight. Then she hopped out and found the correct elevator—ten through nineteen—got in, reached over, and pressed seventeen. When she finally reached her stop, it was six-eleven.

Not too bad, she thought. *Despite it all. Hopefully, he's still here.*

Chapter 14

Ian was beginning to wonder if Avery would show up. Not simply because being ten minutes late was a big deal but because this meeting had been a long shot, to begin with.

He had already swung by reception to let them know he was expecting Ms. Avery Jensen and to verify he hadn't for some reason missed her.

He had decided he would not give up until six-thirty, so there was time. Still, he couldn't help glancing toward the reception area every few minutes. Finally, he saw a girl exit from the elevators looking flustered. She paused where she stood for a moment to throw back her long, dark hair and catch a quick breath. Then she squared her shoulders and approached the receptionist's desk.

Ian wasn't surprised to see Jane, the *Tribune*'s astute receptionist, size up the girl immediately and ask, "Ms. Jensen?"

"Yes!" Avery said, clearly surprised "How did you know?"

"Oh, just a guess. Ian—I mean Mr. Callahan—said he was expecting someone, so I thought it might be you."

"Oh, great." Avery sounded relieved. "He is still here. Sorry, I am late."

"I will let him know. You can have a seat," Jane said, pointing to the not very comfortable chairs in the front entry. Ian had to chuckle a bit at the way Jane always managed to make visitors feel both relieved and on edge at the same time.

Avery piled her stuff in a seat and sat down next to it as Jane picked up the phone to ring the desk Ian had been camped out on waiting for his appointment, her eyes meeting his on the first ring.

"Ms. Jensen has arrived," she said into the mouthpiece as if he had no idea what was going on.

"Thank you, Jane. Did we really need all the formality?"

"Yes, sir," she said with a smile and hung up the phone again. Turning to Avery, Ian heard her speak again. "He'll be right out."

With a light chuckle, Ian waited for a few beats before he headed up to the front and showed Avery back to a conference room where he'd already set up a few things.

As the two of them sat down to the table, there was a bit of tension in the air. Avery clearly had no idea what to expect, and Ian worked to understand how best to calm her nerves. The anxiety of the moment was unusual for him because Ian had interviewed many people through the course of his career so far and typically felt quite comfortable around people. He rarely got awkward like this. Surely once they got going, things would settle in, and he would find his comfort level.

"Avery, thank you so much for agreeing to meet me," he said. "I wasn't sure if you would reply, but I am so glad to have an opportunity to talk with you. As I mentioned, your post on *The Elusive Heron* describes interactions that I believe are quite unique."

"It's no problem. I actually am really glad to be meeting with such an expert. I think that, because Heron is so discreet with their business interactions, this should be very informative for both of us."

"I think so too. Hopefully, I can provide you with whatever guidance you need."

Things were a little less tense now, but there was still a bit of formality in the air. Although the further they got into their meeting, the more comfortable things got.

"Why don't we start with you telling me in more detail about your experience at Heron? Have you had your second meeting with them already? How did that go?"

The two shot questions back and forth to one another for well over an hour. Ian listened attentively to Avery's descriptions about her meetings, interrupting every once in a while, to ask questions or to try to dig out more details about what she'd heard and seen, what she thought about why some questions were asked or why she thought they seemed to like her so well. He was trying to get any detail that might help him understand why Avery had been treated differently than others.

When asked, Avery was clearly at a loss to know any motivation Heron might have had for her special treatment. She could think of no connection she had with the company, no special talents she might have that some of their existing customers might not possess, no special assets or social standing, no reason for special treatment in any way.

"Unless they're just excited to have a younger group take an interest," she mentioned. "They did say you would need to update your template at least every five years and any time you had some major life event. And it costs money to run a new template."

"That would make sense," Ian said, thinking out loud. "Over the course of your lifetime, you should statistically bring in more dollars for the company than the typical demographic of forty-plus." Something in his voice betrayed his suspicions that there had to be more to it than just that.

During their meeting, Avery asked Ian about Heron's practices, why he has been investigating, and what triggered him to look closer into this particular company, taking her own notes toward her paper.

He said, "When I first started investigating Heron, it was partly because their service was new, and I wanted to inform the public about what they were providing, but as I looked deeper, I could see that behind their motto, *The time you always wanted*, was an agenda that I think the public deserved to be aware of. The practices I have learned of show Heron to be a company that is monetarily and power driven, no matter the expense. They have crushed dreams, made heartbreaking and incomprehensible decisions, and now we have the beginning of a class system based on access to Phase Two."

"Wow!" Avery said. "Is there anything I can do?" She looked surprised to have heard the words come out of her mouth, but Ian was glad to hear them. She was the first person he had heard of being accepted into the program so quickly, and the only one so far who didn't seem to feel the threat of having the company stand against her.

Ian paused briefly, although he had already been trying to figure out how he and Avery could work together. She was in the midst of her induction with Heron, and if she were willing to provide Ian information while completing the process, it would be incredible.

It might not even turn out to be all that detrimental to her, either.

Unlike some of their other customers, she was young enough to make a future for herself away from Heron's influence if needed.

"Do you have another appointment with Heron?" Ian asked in response to Avery's question

"I'm scheduled for my template creation appointment, and they told me I would receive my identification bracelet then."

"Because you are in the midst of interactions with Heron, and they appear to value you particularly as a client, would you be willing to be an informant to me as you continue this process?"

"You mean just continue on with Heron, despite what you have told me regarding their ethics as a company and what effect they are having on society?"

"Ms. Jensen, I truly believe that with you on the inside and able to access first-hand information, we can expose Heron for the company that they are."

"If you really think it will help, I am happy to do what I can."

"Wow," Ian said with a sigh. "Thank you so much. I feel incredibly lucky to have met you. Can you please do your best to document your experience at your next appointment? Then we can meet shortly after and you can brief me as to what occurred."

"So, I'll share this information with you, and you then provide it to the public? Do you think that this puts either you or me at risk due to Heron's apparent power?" Avery asked.

Ian thought more of her for asking the right question, but he'd been hoping she wouldn't. He really didn't have any clear idea of how to answer. He didn't want to scare her, but he felt ethically bound to warn her of the potential risks of talking to the press.

"I cannot pretend there's no risk at all. Heron is a very powerful company. I will have to print articles using pseudonyms, because I have printed too many under my own name at this point, and I promise I won't use your name. I'll do everything in my power to protect your identity, but your experience is unique. I doubt we would be fooling the company, no matter what we do."

He could see the emotions warring across her face. He saw her concern that he had taken her question seriously, instead of brushing it off, and the relief that washed over her when he told her he'd work to protect her identity.

Finally, she nodded. "Yes, I can do that, Mr. Callahan. But I want to know that I am free to back out at any time if I feel I need to."

"Of course, Ms. Jensen. You are under no binding obligation."

She and Ian agreed that she would contact him after her template appointment. As Avery was gathering her things to leave the meeting, she instinctively checked her phone.

"Huh, look at this," she said, turning it to show Ian. On the screen, he could see it was a picture message from someone named Sarah. The picture was of a sign that read "Preferred Customers This Line." Below that in smaller writing, it said, "Phase Two Plan Holders, Employees, VIP Club Members." The message from Sarah read, "Really? Can you believe this!? How was your meeting with Callahan?"

"That is exactly what I am talking about," Ian told her.

Avery nodded again and walked out to the elevators. Ian watched as she started a reply to Sarah, but, a few lines in, apparently decided to call instead.

Avery dialed Sarah as she walked to her car. "Avery! Did you get my message?" Sarah demanded. "This is insane! There was a special freaking line for Phase Two Plan holders at my cell phone store! What is going on?"

"That is totally over the top! But now that I met with Ian from the *Tribune*, it doesn't surprise me so much. This company is bad news."

"Whoa, really?"

"Yes! Really," Avery said with confidence now. "As far as I can tell, they have no ethics and are driven by money. They plan to create an elite class of citizens comprised exclusively of plan holders, and from the looks of the photo you sent, they are well on their way to success."

"So, I gather this means you aren't going to your next appointment?"

"On the contrary actually!"

"What?"

"Ian thinks that it would be the best if I went ahead with the appointment so we would have someone on the inside."

"Ummm…Avery…you're sounding a little crazy. 'We would have someone on the inside?' First of all, who is 'we,' and second of all, is this safe?"

"Right. I get it. This probably sounds insane, but meeting with Ian and hearing about Heron made me realize I have to do this."

"Okay, you are obviously passionate, and I get that. I know when you've made up your mind, you've made up your mind. Can you please tell me what your plan is, so if something happens, I might have a clue what went down and where to look for the body?"

"Sarah, come on," Avery said. "Anyhow, I love that you get me and, yes, I am going to my next appointment and pretend everything is normal."

"Normal. Right."

"I know." Avery realized how far away from any-thing normal she had drifted. "I'm just supposed to pay as close attention as possible and try to recount my experi-ence when I meet with Ian after."

"Can you please call me or text me when you go to your appointment, and when you are meeting with Ian?"

"Sure."

"Is there anything I can do?" Sarah's voice broke. "Anything at all?"

Sarah's concern touched her. "Maybe you can come with me when I meet with Ian," Avery told her. "I'll call you."

"Okay, please do. Please be safe."

"I will." To herself, she said, *I'll try.*

Chapter 15

Ella had returned home, and Katie's hope that things would take a turn for the better had not been realized. In fact, it had been quite the opposite. After a couple of days at home, Ella became sick again, congested, and running a fever. Katie thought it was just a simple cold but remembered what the doctor told her about Ella's weakened immune system. She'd taken Ella to the hospital within a few hours of the first symptoms, but Ella's heath declined rapidly. It was hard for Katie to digest, as everything happened so quickly. Nothing the hospital did seemed to help her daughter.

Katie watched helplessly as Ella's heath continued to worsen and she slipped into a coma. When the doctors notified Katie that the best they could do at the time was to keep her stabilized while they tried pumping antivirals into her to fight the infection, Katie found herself overcome with anger. Had the doctor's *really* done everything they could? Why did the hospital staff work so slowly? Couldn't they move any faster? The thoughts and emotions continued to bubble inside of her until, eventually, the floodgates opened. What started as a few anger-fueled tears led to a full-fledged breakdown. Katie sobbed until her tears and her emotions went from anger and rage to sadness and defeat.

The release cleared Katie's mind. She knew in her heart that the staff had been working tirelessly and doing all they could. She reminded herself that they had been nothing but great to her and Ella. She wasn't really angry with them but rather heartbroken by where she and Ella were.

Katie was broken down. She was exhausted. She was beside herself with worry, and she wouldn't leave her daughter's side even for a moment, although the nurses kept telling her she had to go home for a few hours to take a shower and eat.

The last nurse practically pushed her out of the room. "You should go home now and take care of you," the nurse said after checking Ella's vital signs and seeing that the child was peacefully resting.

"I can't leave her," Katie said from her position in the chair.

"When is the last time you showered, ate a hot meal?" the nurse asked.

Katie had to think about that. Was it Friday? Maybe Thursday? What day did Ella get sick?

"Yes, that's what I thought. You can't remember, can you?" The nurse folded her arms across her chest. "Come here, let me show you something."

Katie didn't know what the nurse could possibly show her in the room that she hadn't already seen a thousand times since Ella had been admitted. But the nurse was insistent, and Katie joined her near the door to the restroom. The nurse put her arm around Katie's shoulders and led her inside to face the mirror. What Katie saw there was a wreck of a woman, a ghost of herself.

"Is this how you want your daughter to see you?" the

nurse asked after allowing Katie a moment of shock.

"I—I really haven't been paying much attention," Katie said lamely.

"We haven't seen any change with Ella's condition in some time. You should consider going home, eating some real food, not hospital cafeteria fare. Take a shower, change your clothes. We will call you immediately if there are any changes."

Katie realized she hadn't been taking care of her own personal needs much lately, and she didn't want to leave Ella for any reason at all, but she knew the nurse and all the others were right, even though she hated to admit it. It never was going to feel like the right time to leave as long as Ella was in the hospital, but Katie knew she couldn't just keep going on forever as she had been.

However, when she started to leave, Gail at the receptionist station wouldn't allow her to go.

"You shouldn't be driving with no rest," she insisted. "Let me call you a cab."

Katie allowed Gail to fuss over her a little. She really was tired and probably wouldn't be safe behind the wheel. Besides, it felt nice to let someone else do the worrying and make the arrangements for a change.

When she arrived home, she instinctively grabbed the mail on her way in and sat down on the couch to flip through. Without realizing it, within the time it took to go through the first two pieces her body surrendered to the fatigue. After waking under a small pile of mail hours later, she took a long shower, turning up the hot water for as long as the water heater provided. For a long time, she just stood in the heat of the water and wished it could wash all of her concerns away. For those moments, she was able to just be in the shower and not really think about or feel anything.

After standing there with the water beating down on

her, she became aware of the telephone ringing in the next room.

She would normally let the phone simply go to voice mail, and she'd check it later, but nothing was normal when you had a child in the hospital. In this situation, the phone in its most quiet moments was a source of extreme anxiety, and its rings were like a fire alarm warning of imminent danger. The ringing jolted her back into awareness. She punched off the water and jumped out of the shower, still soaking wet. Pausing only for a second, she grabbed a bathrobe on her way to the phone, trying to tug the robe around her wet skin as she went.

Finally, she reached her purse and frantically rummaged through it searching for the source of the ringing. After the fourth ring, she managed to swipe the phone on and said "Hello" before it even reached her ear.

"Ms. Sullivan. This is Tina, and I am calling on behalf of Dr. Nichols."

Even before Tina had gotten to her name, Katie's heart had sunk. She'd heard that tone of voice before, the clinical detachment that nurses got in their voice in order to help them deliver bad news.

"Yes?" Katie said tentatively, sinking down on the edge of her bed as she did. *Please don't let it be very bad,* she thought. *Please just let it be a small thing. Please, please, please.*

"It would be best if you returned to the hospital immediately."

Katie had already begun running around grabbing her clothes, pulling on her pants, tears streaming down her face, before she and Tina had finished the call. Understanding she'd been driven home by a taxi earlier, Tina assured Katie she already had one on its way to pick her up.

Katie was angry that she had agreed to take a taxi, because she was worried it would slow her down in getting back to Ella, but was grateful that the hospital staff was willing to help her out some. She was also starting to beat herself up a bit about leaving at all, although she didn't have much time to berate herself since she was so focused on returning to the hospital. Before she knew it, the taxi was out front, honking its horn.

She got the money ready to pay the driver while they were on the way because she wanted to be able to jump out and get in to Ella.

When the cab stopped in the loading zone at the hospital, she attempted to hand the taxi driver two twenty-dollar bills which was far too much for the ride, but she didn't care and certainly didn't want to wait for change.

He wouldn't take the cash, though. "Go," he said. "Nurse said you've got a little girl waiting on you."

His statement probably terrified her more than anything so far. With barely a thank you, Katie made her way through the automatic sliding glass doors and started the journey to Ella's wing. She was jogging at times intermixed with a few steps of walking. Her thinking was that no employees would tell her to stop running if she mixed in a bit of walking.

When she reached Ella's wing, the nurses who knew Katie well looked up at her with sympathy in their eyes.

When Katie reached Ella, a nurse was in the room. Katie had watched Ella's condition worsen. Her daughter had struggled with one illness after another and was having a harder and harder time fighting them off. Even though Katie had seen Ella's condition slowly deteriorate, she'd always had hope that things would get better. Today, Katie recognized a significant difference in the situation.

Ella's clammy skin had become darker, grayer. Katie

stood at her bedside, held her hand, and stroked her forehead. After Katie had a few moments with Ella, the nurse indicated she wanted to speak with her in the hallway. The two walked out, and Dr. Nichols was already outside.

"Katie, I am so sorry, but Ella is just not able to fight off the infection this time," he said. "She has fought a good fight, but her body just doesn't have the strength."

Dr. Nichols continued discussing Ella's change in breathing as a sign of her body shutting down. Katie stood stunned as the painful words met her ears. She watched the short, rapid rise and fall of Ella's small chest through the window and caught her own breath when she saw Ella's chest freeze in place. She was reassured when Ella's breathing started again but was still frightened about what it meant that her breath remained so short and shallow.

The nurse had the deepest sympathy in her eyes as she took hold of Katie's arm before delivering the confirming news. "You can stay with her here. But you need to know the end is near."

Tears streamed down Katie's face. She wasn't hysterical but wondered if maybe this is what they meant by being in shock.

The nurse led her back into Ella's room, and, as she did, Katie realized that she did not want to be in this state of despair during her final moments with Ella. She did her best to compose herself, which involved wiping her face with her sleeve and finishing off with a few large sniffs to pull herself together. Once they were back by Ella's bedside, the nurse sat Katie down in the chair next to the bed, touched Katie's shoulder gently, and walked out.

Katie sat next to Ella's bed and, at first, just held her hand and stroked her forehead, telling her daughter how much she loved her. Then she began to tell her stories, recounting Ella's childhood and the fun times she and Ella had had together.

"Remember when we went to the carnival in the country, and you won that huge bear and carried it around through the entire place even though it was at least as big as you were?" she told Ella, remembering how her little girl was so proud of that prize and determined to carry it around herself. She thought back to how Ella tried carrying it in every way possible and ended up with it sitting on her shoulders like a child.

Katie cried a little during the stories but not too much, and they really were tears of joy as she recounted what an amazing child Ella was. She had no idea whether Ella could hear her voice or her stories, but she remembered how the nurses in the past had told her that even in a coma, people could connect to the voices of people they loved. Katie hoped Ella would at least know her mother was with her and would not leave her side.

Through the long hours, Ella never woke up, never gave Katie any indication she was in there and listening. Finally, around midnight, Katie realized the time had come for her to let her daughter go. "Ella, you have fought such a brave fight," she whispered. "I am so proud of you. You are so strong, and you have given me so much to hold onto. We have had such good times together that I will always cherish." She struggled not to break down before she got everything out. "I don't want you to leave me, but I don't want you to hurt anymore. It's time, honey, for you to take the next big adventure. It's okay, darling, for you to want to go. I will always love you. I will always think of you. Someday we can be together again."

Not trusting herself to say anything else, Katie put her head down on top of Ella's limp hand as she held it in her own. Katie sat with Ella, the two of them together, as they almost always were, until the end.

Sometime after one in the morning, Ella's hand jerked in Katie's, squeezing it one last time before her body lost the fight.

Katie didn't move as the machines started sending their alarms. She just stayed holding Ella's hand, blinded by tears, until the nurses arrived. She felt more than saw as one of them wrapped a strong arm around her shoulders and pried her hand away from Ella's, and, eventually, she was helped up and led out of the room.

Chapter 16

Ian had spent some time processing the meeting with Avery. He was having a hard time believing that his investigations into Heron had led him this far, and now he would not just have stories from after the fact but real-time, moment-by-moment information. As he had worked in the days following the meeting, he found himself wanting to call Katie.

He wasn't sure exactly why, and he wasn't sure what he thought of it, so he was trying not to, as long as possible. He tried to put it out of his mind, but eventually, he just dialed.

He was fairly certain this was overstepping some boundaries, but he took the leap nevertheless.

"Ian?" Katie answered, not sounding so great.

"I just wondered how you were doing."

"Oh, Ian," Katie said, her voice gaining a little more strength, giving Ian just enough courage to plunge in.

"I know it is a bit unconventional for me to phone under these circumstances, but I know how hard of a time you have been having, and how you feel about The Heron Company, so I thought you might like to know that I have found someone who is in the induction phase with Heron, and this person has agreed to provide us information."

Ian didn't realize it, but he had said, "provide *us* information" when certainly he should have said "provide *me* information."

Katie didn't notice, either. Her voice took on a bit of steel as she crisply told him, "Ian. That is wonderful for your investigation. I hope whatever they're doing, you'll be able to expose it. Ella—Ella—" Her voice broke, and Ian felt sick. "Ella is gone. Ian, I just can't stop thinking that I would still have her—" Katie stopped for a moment as her voice broke again. "—if Heron had given her a plan. I don't see myself as a mean or vengeful person, I am just so angry. I could have still had Ella with me—"

"Oh, Katie. I am so sorry to hear about Ella." Ian didn't know what else to say.

"Thank you."

After a brief moment of silence, Katie said quietly, "Ian? Do you think your informant could find Ella's file?"

Ian knew Katie was desperate and deeply grieving, but he also knew that this was too invasive for so early in the process. After all, it would mean breaking the law. As such, it was too much of a risk for Avery just yet until they could gain enough evidence to obtain protection under whistleblower laws.

"Well, I only just met with the insider, so, at this point, I am just asking for a play-by-play of their meetings with Heron, but I will be meeting with them next week. We can plan our next steps then," he told her.

Ian didn't want to leave it at that. He sensed that in her own way Katie had just reached out for a lifeline. He wanted to say, "Why don't you come to the meeting?" but he couldn't risk exposing the anonymity of his source, especially after he'd just promised he'd protect it at all costs. For a moment, he considered that he might be able to involve Katie in his investigation in other ways that wouldn't involve taking her to the meeting but realized their friendship was still too new and her grief too fresh for her to be comfortable working one-on-one with him alone. If he really wanted to give her a chance to be involved, he would have to bring her in on his main source.

"Maybe I can ask my source if they would be all right with your coming to the meeting with me if you're feeling up to it," he suggested. "Then maybe we can all talk about how this might progress. How does that sound?"

She hesitated and finally said, "Okay. So, you will call then?"

"Yes. Is there anything I can do for you, Katie?"

"No."

"Are you going to be okay?"

"I don't know."

While Ian was deeply concerned for Katie, he wasn't sure what the correct protocol was for how he should support a woman he just met who just lost a child. He knew she was dealing with the unimaginable, dealing with the loss of a child and holding it together enough to make the necessary arrangements. He was in awe of what she had gone through in her life. While he had initially been attracted to her courage, he now found himself attracted to her strength.

Ian wasn't exactly comfortable thinking such thoughts. He was a happy bachelor with no intentions to change that status any time soon. As a full-time journalist, he was married to his work and didn't feel that would be fair to a family, even though his recent successes enabled him to work more normal hours and spend a few too many lonely evenings in his apartment the past year or so.

He did feel bad for Katie, though, and he found himself constantly trying to find ways to comfort her without overstepping the bounds of friendship. He checked in with her often as she made funeral arrangements. It wasn't much, but he wanted to be there to support Katie, and this was the only way he knew. He left it to Katie's boss to console her through the actual funeral but offered his condolences and a shoulder to lean into for a while once the sparsely attended services were finished.

Ian forced himself to focus on the Heron story to keep his mind busy during the days before his anticipated meeting with Avery. The first thing he needed to do was make sure Avery would agree to have Katie accompany them. He wasn't sure she still wanted to, but after seeing how devastated she was, he wanted to give her something to hold onto if he could. He just wasn't sure how to approach the subject with Avery.

Remembering she'd said something about being available most evenings after five o'clock and it was almost five-thirty, Ian decided perhaps his best approach would be to just make the call.

When she answered, she sounded out of breath.

"Ms. Jensen? This is Ian Callahan from the *Tribune*."

"Oh, how can I help you, Mr. Callahan? I'm running late for an aerobics class."

"I'll make it quick then. Do you remember the woman who was kicked out of the seminar?"

"Of course."

"Her daughter died."

"Oh, how sad." Avery really did sound sad to hear the news but clearly puzzled as to why he was telling her this.

"She would like to be a part of the investigative team. In fact, she'd like to be able to come to our meeting so we can work out a strategy together."

"Okay?" Avery said, clearly needing more information.

"I promised I'd protect your identity, and I meant it. I won't bring this woman if you're concerned in any way. I wouldn't even ask except…well, except I think she needs something to hold onto right now."

Avery was quiet for a few moments. Ian spent those moments biting his tongue, wondering just when he'd become so clumsy with words and just how he'd come around to essentially inviting a source to become a member of his team.

"You don't think she'd do anything crazy, do you?" Avery finally asked. "I mean, she did make a big fuss at the seminar, and now she has even more reason to hate the Heron Company. I don't want to be a part of some kind of bizarre vendetta."

"No, I don't think she's like that," Ian told her. "I think she really just needs to get at the truth and, if the truth turns out to be what we suspect, do something to keep it from harming others. She is a law-abiding woman who just wants some real answers."

"Yeah, I guess it's okay," Avery said. "I mean, if I'm really getting some kind of special treatment for some reason, they're obviously going to be able to figure out who ratted on them anyway, right?"

Ian laughed half-heartedly. "Yeah, I guess that's true."

"I might bring my friend, Sarah, too," Avery said. "She's been interested in learning more about what's going on, too, and she likes to be a part of things."

"Sounds good. See you next week."

As he hung up, Ian wondered how he'd managed to turn a simple story into what was starting to feel like a social movement. Although he was glad to have met Avery Jensen, he also tried to be a responsible journalist. He still needed to do his homework on her.

That morning, he spent his down time investigating Avery's background, looking for any kind of obvious flags that would get Heron excited about her. So far, he was not finding anything alarming. Avery was now in college and taking three courses, Science and Society, Pre-calculus I, and English 101. She grew up mostly in a suburban neighborhood and, prior to transferring to New Day Preparatory Academy her junior year of high school, she had attended Bronson High as a model student. The yearbook indicated she was involved as part of the Associated Student Body and a member of both Key Club and Honor Society.

Nothing alarming. He would just do a few last-minute checks on her family, but he was feeling pretty good that nothing concerning had come up thus far. Then he started wondering. The man she called her father was actually a step-father. Whoever the real father was had disappeared when she was only seven, and her mother had remarried a year later. However, there was nothing out of the ordinary about a failed first marriage or Avery's parents other than the absence of the biological father. Ian decided he would do a quick check on dear old dad's identity before chalking the question up as one more mystery to be solved by the team.

"No way!" The words were out of his mouth before he realized he was speaking aloud. Fortunately, no one else was in the room at the time. Ian rubbed his eyes and stared at his screen some more to be sure he was reading things right.

After the shock wore off, Ian verified what he had found by going to a few other websites and more official trusted sources. He sat at his desk for a while then, just gathering his thoughts in an attempt to determine exactly how he wanted to proceed with this newly discovered information. After careful consideration, he decided it would be best to wait until after Avery had her appointment at Heron to discuss this with her. He could not understand why she would not disclose this information right from the start. He'd soon find out, though. But first, he would wait to see if she contacted him for their next meeting. If she contacted him. And if she did, they would discuss her secret whether she wanted to or not.

Chapter 17

When the day for Avery's template appointment at Heron arrived, she was ready to go but also nervous. When she thought about it, she supposed that made sense. Now she was a spy of sorts, something she'd never done before, and she would be spying on a pretty darn powerful company. But the way she figured it, she wasn't doing anything wrong. She knew Heron wouldn't see it that way, but she didn't understand why Heron had to be so secretive. Why couldn't people know what was going on? It seemed to Avery that a little transparency really couldn't hurt anyone.

Avery tried to push any nervousness out of her mind and head to her appointment. She selected a fairly casual outfit that still looked very nice. She had on a pair of gray slacks with a modern fit, a yellow cotton loose-fitting blouse, and a white cashmere cardigan that she wore open. It hung fairly long, down to her hips, and she hoped she didn't look as confused and distracted as she felt.

Not surprisingly, she found herself rushing out the door but did manage to get to the Heron complex on time. As she walked from her car to the building, she told herself, "Remember to pay attention. Try to look around. Don't act weird."

She arrived at the large frosted green glass sliding doors and was not surprised to see Malia waiting in the large entry. Avery noted that while it was nice to be greeted, she did find it quite odd that it was always Malia, and that she was always there waiting, standing in the middle of the entry when Avery arrived.

If she had arrived later, would Malia have continued to stand in the same spot until she arrived? Or was she off somewhere else and alerted by security that Avery was arriving before she took her position?

Avery's thoughts were interrupted when Malia spoke.

"Hello, Ms. Jensen. Welcome to your template appointment. How do you feel?"

"Great, thank you," Avery said, even though her knees were shaking and her voice was clearly unsteady.

"Excellent. Tyson and the template team are ready for you."

Malia began walking, apparently expecting Avery to follow.

As Avery walked along behind Malia, she looked around and tried to take in the environment. There really was nothing particularly unusual about the building thus far. She did think that the entry was surprisingly empty each time she arrived, considering the number of cars in the parking lot.

Malia stopped at a white door that had a pad next to it. Avery recalled another door had this same pad, and just as before, Malia swiped a key card in front of the pad to open the door and indicated to Avery that she should enter.

All right then. Avery stepped into the room and saw that she was in some sort of medical type facility. As she entered, she realized she was standing on a metal platform that led to some stairs down to a room beneath the platform.

A few people in Heron-issued lab coats, with the signature three-quarter sleeves, moved around. Although she couldn't see from where she was standing, she imagined that they were all wearing Phase Two bracelets.

She heard a voice she recognized as Tyson from the previous meeting say, "Avery! Welcome to your template appointment. Are you excited?"

"I guess so," she replied.

Tyson had been approaching Avery and was now making his way up the last few steps. "I remember you were eager to get your bracelet, and today is the day. I am sure you are thrilled."

Avery thought for a moment, and she realized that, even though she now felt that Heron was a bad company, there was part of her that still was glad she was getting that bracelet. She kind of hated herself for it, but she knew it was there. She would try to focus on her task of gathering information and hope that somehow the fact she was trying to expose information about Heron would balance out the fact that she would be a little happy to have the bracelet.

Finally, she smiled at Tyson and sighed. "Yeah. I guess I am."

"Well, you should be. You are one of the lucky ones."

This comment did not sit well with Avery. She thought about the woman she would be meeting soon and the little girl she would never meet because that little girl wasn't one of the lucky ones. Avery didn't like the fact that there were "lucky people" and "unlucky people," and that pulled her from her moment of excitement.

"Let's head downstairs and get you ready."

"All right," Avery said but actually was wondering what it meant to "get ready."

When they reached the bottom of the metal staircase, Tyson said, "Please go into this room. In there, you will find a robe and a paper blanket. Please remove all of your clothing and put on the provided robe, opening in the back. When you are ready, please come out with the blanket in hand. You may leave your clothes in the room."

"All right," Avery said, looking around at the number of people in the room, a good half of which were men.

She followed directions, headed in, and found herself in what looked like a typical doctor's examination room. On the examination table was, as promised, a robe and a paper blanket.

She began to remove her clothing and set it on the chair near the table. She put on the robe, opening in the back, and tried her best to cover up. She was pleased that at least the robe overlapped in the back so she wouldn't have to walk around exposed.

After she was ready, she took a moment not only to look around but also just to relax. She didn't notice much unusual about the room. She did see advertisements hanging on the wall.

Escape Resorts. All of our resorts around the world are now exclusive Phase Two resorts. Come enjoy Escape.

Tired of waiting in line at your financial institution? Elite Financial offers our Phase Two Plan holders our signature service. No lines. No fees. No hassle. Elite. Because you deserve it.

Wow, Avery thought. *Crazy.*

She headed out of the room, opening the door quietly and slowly.

Tyson was waiting. "Great! Let's head over," he said.

Tyson led Avery a short distance over to a group of men near what appeared to Avery to be an MRI machine. Avery was very conscious of what she didn't have on just then.

"Avery. This is our template team. They will guide you through the rest. I will be observing from there."

Tyson pointed up to a room that was looking down on where they were standing. There was a large window that would allow observers to clearly see the goings on of the room. It didn't make Avery feel any better to realize she would actually be the subject of an observation deck while lying there naked except for a flimsy bit of paper.

"All right. Thank you," was all she said, feeling intimidated.

Tyson headed up to the room.

One of the members of the team, a tall blond man wearing one of the freshly pressed three-quarter sleeve lab coats, outstretched his hand to introduce himself.

"Hello, Avery. I am Warren, the lead of the template team. Nice to meet you."

"You, too," Avery said with a small smile, keeping her hands on the paper robe instead of reaching out for a handshake like normal.

"Are you ready?" Warren said.

"I think so."

"You'll be great."

Warren began with instructions while the other members of the team dispersed and headed off to do…whatever…Avery couldn't even begin to guess.

"Shortly, a table will emerge from this tube. When it is out, please lie down with your head closest to the tube.

Remove your robe and place the sheet over yourself. Once you are ready, we will begin. Do you have any questions?"

"Actually, yes," Avery said. "What will happen after that?"

"We will provide you a sedative so you will not move or be uncomfortable during the template process. The table will enter the tube. We will make your template, place it on file, and you will be moved to recovery. You may feel a bit groggy at first but will then be ready to get your bracelet and head home."

"Simple as that?" Avery said with a hint of sarcasm.

"Simple as that," Warren replied with confidence. "Shall we proceed?"

"I'm ready," Avery said.

She situated herself on the table, looking around to see who was watching. A glance up and she saw Tyson looking down at her. She did her best to cover up with the blanket while taking the robe off underneath it to preserve as much of her modesty as she could under such circumstances.

Once she was in place, she heard a voice from behind her.

"Avery, we are going to sedate you now."

"All right," Avery said and took a deep breath.

A team member wiped Avery's arm clean and then said, "You will feel a slight prick here." He poked the end of the needle in and administered the sedative.

Warren continued to talk. "We're going to begin to move the table into the tube. We'll see you when the process is complete."

Avery heard what Warren was saying, but things were getting blurry. She did see the outline of Tyson looking down at her and felt the table moving in, but that was the last she remembered.

The next thing she recalled was hearing, "She's conscious."

Then Avery heard the voice of the team leader, Warren, saying, "Avery, your template is complete and on file. Please continue to lie down until you feel ready to move. Your robe is next to you, so when you are ready, you can get up. Tyson will help you find your clothing and then will take you to your bracelet fitting."

"All right," Avery mumbled.

Avery lay there for a while and tried to take in what had just occurred.

She was looking forward to talking to Ian, even though she had no idea what had happened to her while she was supposedly in the tube. She wasn't sure she had much useful information, but she was happy to have someone to share it with and happy if she was helping the cause in any way.

Her eyes were open now, and she could see that Tyson was waiting for her. He was seated right near her.

"How are you feeling?" he asked.

"Good, I think," Avery replied.

"Avery, are you ready to get dressed?"

"I guess so."

Tyson handed Avery her robe, stood, and turned his back to her so she could get dressed with some degree of privacy. Even so, Avery spread the robe over her body as well as she could under the blanket, sat up, and tied a cord in the back, removing the blanket as the last step.

Tyson walked over and outstretched his forearm, indicating she could feel free to use it for stability if needed. She did grab on to it to help her stand up. Once she was standing, she loosened her grip but still held on. Tyson led her to the room where she had left her clothes.

"I will wait for you here."

Avery entered the room and sat down. She just sat for a while. Then slowly she reached for her clothes and got herself dressed. She left the robe and blanket in a pile on the examination table, paused to check if she had herself put together correctly, and opened the door.

Tyson was waiting as promised for her outside.

"Let's go get you that bracelet."

Tyson walked Avery up the metal staircase and out the door. They headed down the hall, and Tyson opened another door. This room was either the same room she was in for her compatibility meeting or a very similar one. In fact, once she entered, she could see the members of her compatibility team.

"Ms. Avery Jensen!" one said, "We're so very pleased that you're here."

Avery walked in toward the table where the panel was sitting in the empty room, and Tyson stayed behind.

"Please have a seat."

Avery reached the table and sat down opposite the panel.

A team member opened what looked like a jewelry box. Avery thought it looked to be the size of one that might hold a necklace. However, inside she saw the silver Phase Two bracelet.

The members began to speak in a formal, coordinated cadence. "Ms. Avery Jensen. We, your compatibility team, deemed you fit for Phase Two and now proudly present to you your Phase Two bracelet."

Avery outstretched her arm, suddenly feeling like she was the proud new initiate involved in a sacred ritual. One panel member held the bracelet ends around her right wrist keeping the links near one another. A second team member hooked a gadget around the two links at the end of the bracelet. He squeezed the arms of the gadget together, which were like a single-hole punch, and released it. Avery could see that it had created a link to bind together the two ends of the bracelet, so no latch was utilized.

One by one each panel member said, "Welcome."

Avery assessed this meant "Welcome to Phase Two," the "ceremony" was over, and it was time for her to go. She got up and headed toward the door.

Tyson was outside. "Well? May I see?"

Avery scooted up her sleeve and showed him.

"You are going to want to show that thing off. Don't want to waste it by having it all covered up," Tyson said.

Avery smiled at him, and said, "Of course," hoping that hid her thoughts.

"We have sent you a list, via email, of our partner companies that support and value our Phase Two Plan holders."

"Thank you," Avery said.

Tyson walked her to the exit. "We are here for you, if you need something. Remember, you must update your template every five years, but for an additional fee for each update, you may do so as often as you like."

"I understand. Thank you."

They two reached the door, Avery said goodbye to Tyson, and left. She walked to her car to head home, but she was not back to her usual self quite yet.

Chapter 18

Ian found himself thinking of Katie often. He felt she might need a friend right now, but he didn't know quite how to reach out to her through her grief. Surviving the loss of a child, he had heard, was one of the most difficult challenges any parent could ever face.

Just finished appointment. When can you meet?

Avery's text message came like the answer to his need.

How about tomorrow at six?

He couldn't get his fingers to respond fast enough. He just had to call.

"Oh. Hi," Avery said when she picked up.

"I thought this might be easier. Do you mind?"

"No. I literally just finished my appointment and am just sitting in my car in the parking lot."

"Are you okay?" he asked, mostly to give him time to check an incoming text message in case it was from Katie.

"Yes, though I wanted to ask you something." She paused for a moment.

"All right," Ian said, ready to give his attention to

Avery now that he saw the message wasn't important.

"I can't take my bracelet off."

"If you're looking for jewelry advice, I'm the wrong man."

"No, the Phase Two bracelet. I can't take it off. There is no latch."

"I think I'm missing something."

"Your friend, the one who lost her daughter, will she be angry with me if I have it on? I don't want to make her feel bad or look like I'm trying to flaunt that I got a plan when she couldn't."

"Her real name is Katie Sullivan, and I think I understand what you're saying. I know Katie is very upset and wants to take action to make sure other children like Ella are given a chance even though Ella wasn't. I understand fully if you don't feel comfortable with her there, but I don't think she would hold it against you that you have a plan."

"No, I'm not worried about me. I remembered you said her daughter just died, and I didn't know how she was feeling."

"Honestly, I think she's devastated. Her entire world revolved around her daughter. But I think it would do her a lot of good to get involved, and I think she wants to be."

"You trust her, I assume?"

"Absolutely."

"Well, sounds good then. Have her come along. Why not?"

"Thank you, Avery. Shall we meet at Brio near my office, so it's a bit more comfortable for everyone?"

"I think that will be just fine. See you then."

Now that he was off the phone with her, Ian realized he was still slightly concerned over his findings about Avery and her connection to Heron. He kicked himself a bit for not bringing it up just then, but he forgave himself as he considered this was something he wanted to address in person. As a reporter, he'd learned there were some truths about people you could only get in face-to-face interaction.

But now he had to consider whether their next meeting together would be the appropriate time if he managed to get Katie there. He'd told Avery he trusted Katie, and he did, but he didn't really know her all that well and couldn't explain why he felt such trust. Every reporter instinct in him said it was a bad idea to bring Katie into this. She was obviously compromised in her opinions, and that opened him up to accusations of biased reporting. But every human cell in him was interested in doing anything he could to bring them together again. His compassion also had him convinced Katie needed a purpose to give her life meaning without Ella.

With a sigh, he realized he was likely going to have to confront Avery in front of Katie. He would just have to trust that Katie would be able to control herself. It would be a good test to see how open-minded she was and exactly how determined she was to help him with his investigation. He was hoping there was a reasonable explanation for Avery omitting her information the last time they talked, but he certainly couldn't guess what it might be.

Moments after getting off the phone with Avery, he called Katie. He was happy that Avery was still agreeable to having Katie to joining them. Now he had an excuse to see Katie again. He had been wondering how she'd been holding up.

Ian called Katie when he knew she was usually home. The phone rang and rang before it finally went to voicemail. This concerned Ian somewhat, but he decided everyone had errands and things to run. It probably wasn't time to worry yet.

"Hi, Katie. It's Ian. I mentioned to you that I was meeting with an informant, and I would see if you could come to our next meeting. The informant, a young woman, has agreed. We are meeting tomorrow at Brio at six. I hope you can make it. Give me a call either way. I hope you will come." Ian was sorry he didn't get a chance to speak to Katie directly but was hopeful she would at least call him back.

He expected to hear from Katie later that evening, but when he had yet to hear from her by the next morning, his head began to spin a bit. He hoped everything was okay with her.

He really had no idea how someone was supposed to deal with the death of their child or what they would naturally do.

He tried to decide if it was all right for him to call again prior to meeting with Avery. Even though he hadn't fully convinced himself it was okay, he decided to go ahead and call just before his normal lunch hour.

He was a bit surprised when Katie actually answered just before the machine came on again.

"Oh! Katie!" Ian said, shocked a little at how lifeless her voice sounded. "Are you all right?"

"No," Katie said bluntly responding with no additional information.

"Oh. Is there anything I can do for you?" Ian asked, not really sure the appropriate way to respond to her.

"No, Ian. There isn't," Katie said matter-of-factly.

"Katie, I am so sorry—" Ian began, but she cut him off.

"Ian, did you need something?" she said, clearly wanting him to get off the phone.

"I left you a message about a meeting I have with that informant, and she agreed it would be okay for you to come."

"Yeah, I got your message," Katie said with no hint that she intended to come.

"I really think it would be great for you to join us," Ian pressed. "I would love to have you there, and we'll be finding out more about Heron. Do it for Ella."

Ian knew all this was a bit over the top, but he knew Katie needed some serious motivation to even consider going. Even if Ella wouldn't have cared if Katie got involved in this project, he knew Katie's daughter wouldn't have wanted her mother to waste away from grief.

"I'll think about it," Katie responded after a few moments.

Ian would take it. That was better than a no. "Okay. Please do. I'll call you to check in when I'm heading down there. Katie, it will feel really good for you to get out of the house and to be working on this Heron project."

"I know," Katie said in a somber tone.

"I'll call you around four," Ian said, sounding enthusiastic and hopeful.

"Okay. Bye."

After hanging up, Ian couldn't let go of the hopeless, lifeless sound of Katie's voice. The more he thought of her being alone with such grief, the more convinced he became that she might need some help.

By four p.m., he found himself pulling up in front of her house instead of getting on the phone as planned. It wasn't until he was standing on her doorstep that he seriously questioned whether this was a wise idea.

He was surprised by the woman who opened her door. It looked as if she'd made an effort to get cleaned up but had used up all the energy she had left in the process. Her hair was still dripping wet, but it was smoothly combed out. She was wearing jeans and a black top but no makeup. Her eyes remained puffy and rimmed with red.

On first sight of her, Ian couldn't help himself. He stepped forward into the doorway and wrapped Katie in a hug. He had no other intention at that moment than to offer her comfort and strength. "I was in the area and thought I'd drop in to check on you," he said, feeling at a loss for what to say.

"Thank you, Ian."

After only a moment, she backed up and led him to the couch. Looking around, Ian could see visible signs of Katie's struggle. The house was clearly lacking attention, and her listless body language had him even more worried.

"Listen, Ian, I'm not sure I'm going to go to your meeting tonight," she said, her voice still sounding hollow.

"I would understand if you didn't," Ian responded, thinking desperately for reasons this woman needed to get out of the house. He had a strange feeling this was a make or break decision for his new friend. She would either decide to keep living and fight, or she would decide to curl up on her couch and drown herself in grief. Katie was a strong woman, and he didn't think she was contemplating anything like overt suicide, but he worried at the loss of light in her eyes and life in her voice. He knew it was possible for a person's spirit to die while their body kept walking, and he didn't want that to happen to Katie.

Not coming up with any answers, he finally looked up into Katie's eyes and saw the pleading look they held. Hope ignited in him as he realized Katie, on the inside, was begging for someone to help her get out, help her figure out how she was supposed to respond, how she was supposed to keep living without Ella at her center.

"I—I think it would be incredibly hard to go through losing your child," Ian started, not knowing just what he was planning to say. "And I don't know what you're supposed to do now. But I don't think Ella would have wanted you to stay home and do nothing. I think she would want you to get back to living as soon as you could, whatever you think that should be."

Katie nodded as if he was telling her things she'd been trying to talk herself into.

Ian stood up to allow her time to think about things. He knew from working with accident victims that sometimes people still feeling shock could take a little longer than normal to process things. Katie had that same look about her. He decided to clean up her kitchen while she thought.

"You're right," she finally said. She grabbed a dish towel and started drying the dishes Ian left on the rack. "Ella never knew there had been a chance for her, or that some company decided to take it away. But she was proud to have a strong mommy. I can't let her down by sleeping all day."

"So, you'll come to the meeting tonight?"

"I think I will. I think you're right. It'll be good for me."

"Oh, I'm so glad. We're meeting at six at Brio."

"That's an hour away."

"If you want, I can help you around here a bit, and we can ride together," he said.

"No. I think I need to do some things on my own." Katie looked around with some distaste at the messier-than-normal state of her house. "But I'll be there."

Ian was surprised but pleased that Katie would be joining the meeting, and he understood her desire to put things straight on her own. For a woman like Katie, getting her external environment in shape was one way she

helped herself get her internal life in shape. After confirming one more time that she didn't want his help before the meeting, he excused himself and headed back to
his office.

Chapter 19

For once, Avery managed to get to Brio on time for her appointment with Ian. Maybe Phase Two was starting to have an effect on her, making her more responsible somehow, she thought. Between signing binding contracts for significant monetary sums and meeting with newspaper reporters, she was feeling more grown-up than just a simple college freshman.

The hostess had informed her that her party was out on the patio, but was distracted helping a larger family get settled, so Avery made her way out alone.

As she wandered through the tables trying to find Ian, she couldn't help but notice the three-quarter sleeve fashion most of the customers were flaunting as if they were something special. It was starting to make her angry until, finally, she saw Ian sitting at an empty table for four with a number of papers spread out in front of him. When their eyes met, he stood up and extended his hand.

"Avery, I'm so glad you made it. Isn't your friend joining us?"

"Yes. She will be here shortly. And yours?"

"Same," Ian said, "It's good to see you."

"Did you see these people?"

Ian looked confused for a moment, but as his eyes drifted quickly around the patio, understanding took over. At a table to the left, three people were taking pains to flash their Phase Two bracelets in the sun.

To the right, there were two women in workout clothes specially designed to make the Phase Two bracelets stand out.

"Wow!" Ian said quietly. "I didn't realize that they made three-quarter sleeve business suits or workout clothes. Quite the fashion trend."

"Seriously! I don't get it!" Avery said. "Why not short sleeves? They already make those. I would still be able to see their fancy bracelet." She self-consciously checked to ensure that her cardigan sleeve covered hers.

"I guess, this way, you can tell one even from a distance," Ian said.

"Maybe."

"Actually, Avery, I'm glad we're both here first. I need to talk to you about something," Ian said with a tone of seriousness.

"What is it?" Avery wasn't sure she liked the intensity she saw in his eyes just then, but he seemed willing to talk it out, whatever the problem was.

"Well, I was doing some routine—"

Just as Ian started his sentence, Katie walked up to the table.

"Katie!" Ian interrupted himself. "I'm so glad you made it. Avery, this is Katie. Katie, meet Avery Jensen."

They shook hands. Avery could see that Katie was doing her best to pull it together. She wore no makeup, her eyes were red-rimmed, and her hair had been air-dried without styling. Avery tried her best to make it seem as if she didn't notice.

After a bit of small talk, Avery couldn't wait any

longer. "Ian, you wanted to ask me something just before Katie arrived."

Ian was still nervous about delving into this line of questioning with Katie there, but now that he'd brought it up, it was now or never.

"Katie, sorry, I just have a few things I need to clear up with Avery. I hope you don't mind."

"No. I'll be fine."

Katie pulled out a menu and propped it in front of her face, maybe even actually reading it.

"Well, what I have to ask is a bit personal. Do you mind?" Ian asked, with a gesture toward Katie.

"Not sure," Avery said, but then again, if it was as serious as he was acting, maybe she wanted a witness. "But go ahead."

"Whenever I meet a new informant, it is routine to do a background check." Ian paused.

"Yes," Avery was getting annoyed. Why would she be worried about this at all?

"Avery, in your background check, I found out that your biological father is Reuben Wilkins." Again, Ian stopped as if that was supposed to mean something profound to her.

"Yes," Avery said. "I know who my biological father is."

"Why would you not tell me this?" Ian burst out, obviously exasperated.

"Why would I? What would that have to do with any of this?"

Ian stared at her for a moment with his jaw hanging open. "Really? You don't know?"

"I guess not."

"Reuben Wilkins is the CEO of Theta Technologies!" Again, Ian stopped as if that would explain everything.

"I know that," Avery said. She could tell that Ian was exacerbated, but she couldn't guess why he might be. Before Ian could explain further, Avery saw Sarah at the patio entry looking around for their table. "Sarah," she called out, relieved her friend was there to help her.

Avery gave Sarah a little wave over to the table and made the introductions all around.

As Sarah took her seat, Avery said, "Ian is asking about my father."

"Marshall?" Sarah asked.

"No. Reuben," Avery answered.

"Ohhhhh," Sarah said, "Bad subject."

"Why? What do you mean?" Ian asked.

"Avery and Reuben aren't exactly close," Sarah said. "Why would you bring him up?"

Ian took a deep breath. "Okay, so it sounds like you are very unfamiliar with Heron and Theta's relationship," he said, sounding a little annoyed but the tension in his face had melted away. "Theta Technologies is the primary investor in The Heron Company and is almost solely responsible for The Heron Company coming to fruition."

"Ohhh," Avery said, hearing an echo around the table from the others. "So, you think that might be why I was deemed compatible so quickly?"

"Yes. I certainly do," he said with confidence.

"But I haven't spoken to Reuben since I was in the first grade."

"Clearly, he still thinks of you," Ian said.

Katie, who had been sitting in silence for some time, finally spoke. "Isn't your last name Jensen?" she inquired, obviously confused since the man they were taking about was Wilkins.

"Yes," Avery responded. "We were devastated after Reuben just left us, but my mom found Marshall, and they got married when I was in second grade. They've been together ever since. Marshall Jensen has been my father nearly my whole life, and I am glad to have his name. I don't think of myself as a Wilkins."

"Whoa. Sorry," Katie said, responding to the venom that had laced Avery's voice.

"No. Don't worry about it. It's just how it is," Avery replied, trying to back down her emotions.

Sarah smiled across the table at Avery in support.

"Thank you for clarifying, Avery," Ian interrupted clearly relieved that she hadn't been intentionally hiding that from him. "I am sorry I had to pry into your personal life. I appreciate that you were willing to share, and hopefully, you are still willing to share your experience at Heron yesterday."

"I am," she said, relieved to be changing the subject. "Maybe we should order first, though."

Everyone agreed that sounded good.

The group ordered their meals while Ian, Katie, and Avery shared their experiences dealing with the Heron Company. Ian shared his knowledge of Heron's operations, as he knew it, as well as people's experiences with Heron up through their second appointment. Until Avery, he had yet to find someone farther in who wanted to share more than a small quote.

He mentioned how thrilled and intrigued he was to hear how the template appointment went for Avery and to get a picture of that portion of the process.

Prior to recounting her experience, though, Avery wanted to include Katie in the conversation and to hear more about her negative experiences. She asked Katie to share first.

Katie had a lot of emotion built up that she hadn't been dealing with, so it was good for her to recount her experience, despite the fact that she broke down from time to time during her story and had to compose herself for a few moments prior to continuing. Katie shared her story, from her application to her rejection, to her outburst, followed by the unusual experience with Heron security and the fingerprinting, and then finally with losing Ella recently to her battle with leukemia. She had ups and downs as she spoke to the group, who did not speak but were extremely attentive as she recounted her experiences and emotions.

When she started her story, Katie was speaking softly and with little energy and emotion, drained by her experiences and heartbreak. However, as she proceeded through the story, she became more energized. It was as if she was being reminded that she still had a reason to fight, Avery thought. Katie needed to take on Heron for Ella.

The group could see the transformation in Katie and were moved, not only by her experiences but by the effect retelling them was having on her. Although it was not yet outwardly discussed, they each felt motivated by Katie's story and felt that something must be done.

It was Avery's turn to tell her story, and she felt a little sheepish after Katie's story because hers ended with having a Phase Two bracelet, which was all that Katie had wanted for Ella. As she began, she tried to tell herself that she was with the group before she got the bracelet and she only did this to help gather information. She hoped the group remembered that and would not resent her for having a plan.

She told them the story of the template team and the room with the MRI-looking machine, explaining that she could not remember the procedure itself but did know she was drugged and put inside the tube. She also told them about the advertisements in the dressing room that promised exclusive access and perks for having a bracelet, the bracelet ceremony with the compatibility panel, and that she had been emailed a list of partner companies that supposedly valued Phase Two customers.

After her comment about partner companies and as she finished, Sarah said, "Oh my gosh, have you guys seen those signs in storefronts for Phase Two? There are stickers by the stores' other awards, like their ratings on the internet."

"Oh, maybe. I did see something the other day that looked like that," Ian said.

Katie shook her head. "Crazy!"

Ian said, "Avery, do you feel comfortable forwarding me that list to print? It might be nice for people to see which companies are supporting this inequality."

"Sure. I'm fine with that. Anything I can do to help."

Avery was glad to be able to provide the list since she was a bit worried about her status with the group. She realized it was not just that she had a plan, but now it seemed her father was an important part of the problem. She wanted to make sure she was contributing.

"Great," Ian said.

Sarah, who had been relatively silent due to her lack of experience with Heron, said, "We have to do something. I want to do something—I want to go in. Maybe I can get something on them?"

This outburst surprised the group a bit, in particular, Avery because she knew Sarah to be relatively passive in the past, but the group was immediately on board and ready to talk about what to do. They found themselves motivated to action after sitting through the stories from the group.

The four spent some time telling other things they had heard about Heron, sharing acquaintances' injustices from being without bracelets, examining Avery's bracelet more closely, and talking over the new fashion trends that were becoming more popular recently. One of the big questions they hadn't been able to answer yet was what exactly it took to qualify for a plan. Neither Avery nor Katie had been able to get a glimpse of the charts in front of the compatibility team during their interviews.

Finally, Sarah said, "What if I go to Heron for an appointment? I can try to take photos of the compatibility charts?"

"It's a start," Katie said.

As a team, they agreed that Sarah would try to make an appointment with Heron. She and Avery would work on setting up a way for her to discreetly take photos during the appointment, and they would contact Ian for everyone to reconvene after the appointment.

They left Brio, and Avery could tell that the others were as energized as she was. They were finally taking on Heron.

Chapter 20

Sarah was really excited to be participating, really moved by the stories that were told during their meeting at Brio and surprised by Avery's most recent visit to Heron. Even though she had read some of Ian's articles, hearing him tell them first-hand was particularly powerful. The most impacting for Sarah was Katie Sullivan telling her story.

She filled out the online form for Heron to request an appointment as soon as she got home and made plans with Avery for the following Saturday to shop for some kind of hidden camera jewelry that would let her take a picture even with the members of the compatibility team watching her.

Avery was about fifteen minutes late Saturday for their shopping trip, but Sarah was used to it. She had known Avery for a long time and knew she did things on "Avery time" as Sarah liked to call it.

"Hey—sorry," Avery said, already knowing that her being late was expected behavior.

"No worries," Sarah said. "Are you excited?"

"Yes. How could I not be? Shopping for gadgets,

big-time spy world, here we come! Right?—Hey! Did you hear anything back from Heron after filling out the form?"

"Yeah," Sarah answered, remembering she hadn't texted Avery the news. "I got an appointment and interview on Tuesday at four o'clock."

"Well, it looks like we have some work to do then," Avery said, lowering her voice as if someone might be listening. "You nervous?"

"Not yet. Just excited. But I am sure I will be on Tuesday. I bet you didn't imagine that class paper would turn into this, did you?"

"Oh my gosh, seriously? Who knew?" Avery replied and then refocused on finding their destination. "Where is that store anyhow? Right around here somewhere. I know I have seen it here before," she said somewhat to herself.

"Right there! See it?" Sarah said. "Seriously? It is called Spy Store? Not the sneakiest of names, but, I guess, at least it's to the point."

When they entered the store, they were overwhelmed and temporarily sidetracked by all the gadgets available. They grabbed interesting items off the shelves to show one another. They laughed and joked about how they or others might have used items like night vision goggles or cameras on long flexible rods. They were having a great time, but possibly their behavior was on the edge of obnoxious.

A guy in his early twenties who looked to be at home in the Spy Store, approached and said, "Can I help you two with anything?"

His question came across as sincere, but there was a hint of nerves and some annoyance as well in his voice.

With his question, Avery was reminded why they had come to the store in the first place. She glanced at Sarah, and they quickly composed themselves.

"Yes, actually," she said. "We are looking for a discreet camera."

"No problem," he said, as if he heard similar requests every day. "We have a wide variety of disguised cameras. Follow me."

The employee walked the two over to a nearby section of the store and started pointing out different varieties. "Here we have the clock style cameras—over here, the watch and pen cameras—"

He was interrupted by Sarah. "Okay, right, we're looking for something small like these," she said, indicating the watch and pen cameras.

"Would you like me to help you any further with your decision?" he asked.

The two looked at one another, and Sarah said, "Nah. I think we just need to look at the options and talk it out."

"All right then. Just let me know if there is anything else I can help you with," he said as he left Sarah and Avery to their deliberation.

They quickly eliminated the watch as it was far too manly and ridiculously noticeable when Sarah tried it on.

Although they liked both the pen and the key fob cameras, they weren't certain Sarah would be able to keep those items in her hands throughout her appointment. What they really wanted was something she could pin to her outfit, but the best they could find was a yellow smiley-face pin in which one of the eyes of the face was the camera. Sarah just wasn't certain she could pull off a serious outfit with that pin on it.

The employee walked by, and Sarah stopped him. "Hey, is this the only pin-type camera you have?"

"Yes, in stock, I am afraid it is."

After much discussion and despite the tacky nature of the smiley-face pin, they decided it was the only option. They agreed that Sarah would have to put together an outfit to pull off the pin. The people at Heron didn't know her so she could dress however she chose.

As Avery dropped Sarah off at her place, they high-fived one another, proud of their purchase, and Avery told Sarah to call if she needed any help or advice getting ready for her appointment.

"I will. Thanks," Sarah replied. "I will call you after my appointment for sure."

"Okay," Avery said. "Good luck."

Sarah actually found an outfit she thought might work with the button cam. She had to dig deep into her closet, but she found casual sneakers, navy blue work-wear style pants, a white T-shirt, and a jeans jacket, which was where she put the button cam among her select band buttons. She knew she should dress up a bit more than her outfit of choice offered, but that was a sacrifice that would have to be made to have a chance of getting any photos discreetly.

She woke up early Tuesday and headed to class, bringing along the clothes for her appointment in a gym bag. At school, she tried to stay focused, but she found herself spacing out from time to time during the day, thinking about her appointment, how she should act, and what she should be looking for.

When three p.m. finally arrived, Sarah changed and headed over to Heron.

She was angered by the allocation of the parking stalls in the Heron Company parking lot but not surprised after hearing the stories from the group the other day.

While making the relatively long haul to the Heron building from her parking spot, Sarah realized she was nervous. She was excited though and optimistic that she could manage her nerves appropriately.

As she reached the oversize frosted green glass doors at the entry, they opened to a woman standing just inside, a woman Sarah knew would introduce herself as Malia.

The woman approached and did just as expected, "Hi. You must be Sarah Greenbaum. Welcome. My name is Malia. Heron Induction Specialist."

Sarah was momentarily overwhelmed but then remembered she wanted to be taking photos. She placed her hand into her jacket pocket and found the camera's remote control. She realized she may have looked a little frazzled and distracted as she fumbled briefly for the remote, but she was hoping it wasn't too noticeable and was fairly confident she had regained her composure now. She snapped a few photos of Malia just as the woman was turning away to lead Sarah to her compatibility panel appointment.

Things inside the compatibility panel assessment room went exactly as Avery and Katie had described. Sarah answered the panel's questions the best she could, no matter how unusual they were until the panel finally indicated they would provide a decision within the next forty-eight hours.

Sarah had snapped some photos of the panel during the interview but wasn't sure she'd been able to get anything of the forms on their clipboards as she'd tried to lean over the table and shake each panel member's hand and snap the camera with her other hand.

As she walked out the door, she thought to herself, *Not too bad, Sarah. This spy stuff isn't too difficult after all.*

She expected Malia to be waiting outside, but the woman was not there. Sarah exited the room tentatively and let the door shut behind her but stood in the hall, trying to decide if she should wait or head for the exit.

Sarah caught a glimpse of a man in a Heron uniform before she saw Malia walking briskly toward her.

"My apologies for being a bit late, Ms. Greenbaum,"

Malia said. She gave a pointed look at the man as she passed him. "How was the interview?"

Relieved, Sarah said, "Good, I think."

"All right, then. I will see you out. You will be hearing from the panel, as I am sure they indicated."

"Yes. Thank you. But, do you have a restroom nearby? It's kind of a long drive home."

Malia led Sarah to the restroom, indicated which hall Sarah should take to find Malia when she was through, and left Sarah to her needs. But when Sarah came out, the hallway wasn't empty. The same man she'd seen upstairs was putting screws back into an air vent when she stepped out. He walked toward her then faced the entry security panel on a nearby door. As he slowly accessed his key card, he hoarsely whispered, "You're going to have to be more discreet than this if you're dealing with Heron." He glanced significantly at her smiley-face button cam.

Sarah was embarrassed and flustered, but she did manage to snap a photo of the man and get out, "Oh, uh…what's your name?"

As he swiped his card and entered the room, he mumbled "Lee Park," and disappeared.

Sarah was stunned and really anxious now. She just wanted to get out of Heron and quickly went to find Malia.

Malia led Sarah to the front exit, and Sarah was relieved to get back in the fresh air.

The first call she made when she got back to her car was to Avery.

"Hey!" Avery said.

"Hey."

"I am on my way to the gym. How did everything go?"

Sarah proceeded to tell Avery everything—about

how she froze initially but did get photos, she thought, but she had yet to download and look at them. She also told Avery about Lee Park and hoped Ian would be able to find out more about him.

"Oh, my gosh, Sarah!" Avery said. "That sounds scary. Are you all right?"

"Yeah," Sarah said. "I guess I am. It was scary, but it worked out all right."

"I am glad. Why don't you send the photos to the group, and then we can arrange a meeting for the four of us. How does that sound?"

"Sounds perfect. I'll send over what I got tonight."

"Great," Avery said. "Good work, Sarah!"

It made Sarah happy that she might have obtained some useable information and contributed something to the cause. She buckled up her seatbelt and headed home.

Once she arrived, she headed straight to the computer. Hungry and tired as she was, she really wanted to get this email sent.

She downloaded twelve photos. Two were of Malia, four were of the panel, five showed blurry white shapes on a dark table, and one was of Lee Park. Sarah was frustrated as she looked over the photos. The quality was very poor, and some of the photos did not capture what she intended. She'd known that the pictures of Malia might not be great because she was turning away by the time Sarah took them, but one of those photos turned out to be one of the best in the set. The four photos from the panel were not so good. Two of the photos only captured part of the members' faces. She hoped maybe Ian would be able to use some kind of photo-enhancing technique to pull out more information from the forms the panel had used. But Sarah was the most pleased with the photo of Lee Park. She hoped with his name, workplace, and this photo, Ian could find some information on this fellow.

She sent a little explanation along with the photos.

Hi, everyone
Here are the photos I got with the cam at my Heron appointment. The first two are of Malia, the Heron Induction Specialist, the next four photos are of my compatibility panel. The next five are my attempts to capture whatever was on the compatibility panel's clipboards, and the last photo is of a man named Lee Park who stopped me and warned me to be more discreet. He seemed like he wanted to help. Ian, can you find any information on him?
Thanks. Talk to you soon.
Sarah

She sent off the email and felt satisfied that her job, at least for now, was complete.

Just before heading to bed, Sarah checked her email one last time and was surprised to find an email from Heron. She clicked on it, expecting it to be a follow-up question that the panel needed clarification on, but it turned out to be the panel's decision.

Ms. Greenbaum,
The Heron Company receives far more requests for Phase Two plans than we can grant. Unfortunately, your compatibility score did not meet the expectations of the company. We appreciate your interest in the Heron Company.

Sarah was shocked. First of all, she was not expecting a response so quickly, and second, the response was a *no,* which made her feel strange.

She had been so caught up in her mission that she hadn't thought about the other aspect of her application, how she felt about it, and what her expectations were. Now that it was here, she realized even though she did want to help expose Heron's practices, part of her really wanted to be accepted by Heron. She wasn't exactly sure why, but it could have something to do with the fact that Avery had been accepted.

Chapter 21

The photos Sarah sent over Tuesday evening were almost completely unusable, but Ian didn't want to tell her that. They didn't need images of Malia, having ample evidence the woman worked for the company since she appeared in almost all of Heron Company's advertising and marketing. The images of the papers turned out to be completely illegible when they managed to focus on the papers at all. Of the photos she took of the panel, the angles were difficult to try to identify people from, but it might be possible to start identifying who held positions within the company. The most interesting photo, Ian thought, was the one of Lee Park. Clear and face on, it enabled Ian to conduct some helpful research, and he arranged to meet the little group on Thursday evening, again at Brio.

He was pleasantly surprised when Katie met him just outside his office building that evening. They walked to the restaurant together with Katie telling him about the small steps she was taking to pick up the pieces of her life. They found Sarah already waiting for them out on the patio.

The three talked casually for a while as they waited on Avery. They carefully avoided talking about Sarah's appointment so they wouldn't have to repeat anything. Sarah shared her private classification of "Avery time" with the others, causing Katie to laugh a little for the first time since before Ella died as far as Ian could tell. He tried to keep the conversation light-hearted for a bit longer, but it didn't take long for them to notice some new items on the menu. The choices seemed to take the comfortable corner sandwich shop in a fancier direction, causing Katie and Sarah to start speculating on what could be the driving force behind the sudden move. Before they could take things too far, Ian decided to bring the conversation back to the here and now.

"Maybe I should wait for Avery to tell you this, but since I am not sure when she will get here, I think I will go ahead without her."

The others were clearly intrigued.

"I found Lee Park," Ian said bluntly.

"Really?" Sarah said.

"Lee Park is the man who warned you at to be more careful when dealing with Heron, right?" Katie asked Sarah, demonstrating that she had also read through Sarah's email.

"Oh, wow!" Sarah said to Ian while nodding at Katie. "So, how did you find him?"

"I was surprised it was so easy since most of the names I've found associated with Heron have been almost impossible to discover, but all I needed for him was what Sarah provided—his name, photo, and workplace. Thanks for that, Sarah. Anyhow—" he continued, not quite able to suppress pulling out a dramatic pause. "—I convinced him to meet us here today to discuss further action."

"Really?" Sarah asked.

"That is really amazing, Ian," Katie said. "Do you think he is trustworthy?"

"Well, I can't say for sure, but I do know he is taking risks of his own by meeting with us here today. As you know, Heron is a powerful company that likes its privacy. They may even have a contract in place legally preventing him from talking. At the least, they'll be able to fire him, maybe put him in jail. Because of their connections, it's possible they'll be able to prevent him from getting another job in this city."

"Oh, I suppose he is taking some serious risks then," Katie said, sounding convinced.

The group tried to figure out what Lee Park would be like and what he might have to say to them until Avery finally arrived. She looked a bit disheveled as she hustled over to the table with her purse falling from her shoulder and dangling from her forearm.

"Sorry," she said, out of breath.

She sat down at an open seat, but before she could even get settled, Sarah said, "Lee Park is coming."

"What?" Avery replied.

"Lee Park is coming," Sarah repeated.

"Really? Is he going to help?"

"We don't really know," Ian told her. "We just know that he agreed to meet with us."

"Whoa. When is he coming?" Avery asked.

"Any minute now," Ian said, with a glance at his watch. He had purposely told Lee to meet them half an hour later than he planned on meeting with the others. He'd wanted a chance to prepare them and already had a feeling Avery struggled to arrive for appointments on time. He wanted to be sure they were all there before Lee arrived.

The group decided to order some drinks and appetizers as they waited. After all, it was dinner time, and it would be a welcome distraction from speculations about what Mr. Park might have to offer and having him accidentally hear their talk.

Shortly after the group ordered, Avery noticed a familiar-looking Asian man in his mid-to-late thirties approaching the table with purpose. The intent look on his face clearly frightened her a bit, and her voice came out breathless as she called the group's attention to him. "Is this him? I see someone coming?"

Sarah looked around toward the man Avery indicated and said quietly while trying not to look like she was talking about Lee, "Yup, that's him. He's here."

The man reached the table and stood for a moment.

"Hello, Ian. Hello, Sarah. Hello, Avery, and hello…" He waited for a cue on Katie's name, which she gave him and shook his hand.

Ian could see shock on Avery's face when Mr. Park knew her name, but she didn't comment on her surprise. Ian made a mental note to ask her about her reaction later. Was this a man she knew and was surprised would talk? Ian still wasn't sure what to believe about her and her association with Heron Company, so he was watching her carefully.

Ian continued to watch as Lee Park sat down tentatively and seemed to keep an eye on Avery as he did. While his presence was initially intimidating, as he began to relax, the group soon felt very comfortable with him. It was clear he did not have negative intentions toward their little group, and they did their best to reassure him that they would do all they could to protect him if he was working with them. From time to time, he looked around nervously as if checking to see if there was any indication he was being watched by Heron. His vulnerability was both comforting and upsetting to the group. Because of it, they knew he was no real threat to them but also because of it, they knew Heron probably was.

The group talked openly with Lee about their experiences and their hopes to expose Heron's practices, in an attempt to both inform the public as well as to influence change for social protection. They felt it was imperative to stop the segregation and prejudice which had been setting into their community since the introduction of Phase Two in the market.

Lee let the four speak, listening to all they had to say and expressing his appreciation for their ability to see more of Heron's activities than most people who weren't already involved with the company. But once they finished telling him what they hoped to accomplish, he said firmly, "I'm not sure you realize who you're dealing with. Your little grassroots movement is not even of minor concern to Heron. They have already become too big for that. I can fill you in more on that, off the record, but for what you want to accomplish, you will have to do better, if you want real change. I'm sorry, but you will need to go to a more powerful source."

Lee's tone convinced Ian the man knew what he was talking about. The women were momentarily speechless after Lee's comments, and Ian was thinking he should have known better than to invite him. He'd allowed himself to relax and get carried away with his fascination with Katie, but if he'd been paying more attention, he might have seen the obvious sooner.

He was still kicking himself when Katie said, "Well, what then?" clearly asking for some guidance from Lee.

Lee seemed prepared for her question. "I am not sure you are going to like this," he said as he glanced at Avery, "but I think your only option is to go to your father. He has the kind of influence you need."

Glancing around the table, Ian realized Sarah had already thought of this. Her expression was being tightly controlled, but she watched Avery with a wary eye.

"Right." Katie's voice came from his side, "Avery, you can go to him. Your father is their main financial support."

Understanding from Sarah's watchful eye on Avery that something wasn't quite right, Ian urged caution in his tone as he added, "It might work, Avery. He is the contact we need."

"How do you know who my father is?" Avery asked Lee. Ian noted her eyes had never left Lee's face while the others talked.

"Everyone knows who you are," Lee said with a shrug.

When Avery looked unconvinced, Lee pulled out his phone, tapped it a few times, and then flipped it around to show Avery the screen. Ian leaned over the table to see a picture of Avery on an internal site of the Heron Company called The Heron Family Tree. It was a page dedicated to Reuben Wilkins and included an additional few people on the page, presumably Reuben's parents. While Avery grabbed up the phone to look at the site in more detail, Ian cocked an eyebrow at Lee.

"It's a section of the company site that features all of the important investors and their close family members. They bill it as a way to foster a sense of family, but really it's to be sure everyone is able to recognize any member of the 'family' and treat them accordingly," Lee explained.

"Avery, you don't have to do this," Sarah said.

Ian was both pleased and irritated with Avery's friend. On the one hand, Avery was clearly feeling the pressure with three adults near her telling her to go talk to the man. She needed someone to be on her side. Ian remembered Avery's passion when she talked about her decision to keep Reuben out of her life because he had abandoned her as a child. He imagined contacting her father and asking anything of him at this point would be difficult, especially when he didn't seem to be respecting the boundary she'd set.

But at the same time, they really didn't have a prayer of addressing the inequality of Heron Company's practices without the benefit of someone in power there. Avery was their best option.

"Thanks, Sarah," Avery said, softly, "but I think I do have to."

Ian tried not to show his deep sigh of relief after hearing that and sat patiently as Sarah helped Avery explore her decision fully.

"You don't. We can think of something else."

"There is nothing else," Avery told her. "There is no way we can stop the way Heron awards plans, and the injustice that's occurring as a result. We need him, Sarah. We need his influence." She sounded defeated, but there was a certainty in her voice, letting Ian know she was determined. He could tell the others at the table sensed it too.

"Okay. If you're up to it," Sarah said.

There had still been tension in the group until the decision had been made, but it was released as Avery made her decision. Ian realized he wasn't the only person who had been unsure of Avery's position within Heron. Avery herself seemed to relax some as the rest of the group accepted her dedication to the cause. They were all able to turn their attention more to finishing their meals and chatting casually, feeling more comfortable knowing they had some sort of plan. And hopefully, one that would deliver more satisfying results than what they'd been able to accomplish so far.

Avery seemed to be having some trouble dealing with her decision, pushing her food around her plate and not laughing as freely as she had in the past, but she worked hard to take part in the conversation flowing around her. Whatever happened, Ian knew she would follow through on her decision.

Before they went their separate ways for the evening, Avery agreed she would get in contact with her father at Theta Technologies within the next week and would contact the group after. They thanked Lee Park for his help and guidance. Lee told Ian to feel free to call if they needed anything else.

Overall, Ian thought it was a particularly successful dinner. All things considered, he wasn't sure it could have gone any better, but then Katie surprised him by saying to Ian on the way out, "Ian, would you be interested in joining me for some dessert? I could use an indulgence right now." He could see she was still devastated and certainly not yet ready for any kind of relationship. She was just looking for a little more company this evening, and he was glad to see she was trying to get back to a normal life.

Chapter 22

After the meeting at Brio, Katie was convinced more than ever that something was happening to her community, and she owed it to Ella to make sure that other children not born into the advantaged class had as much of a chance to live as others.

The conversation with Lee Park had been enlightening, not just because of what he had to say, but the way he said it. Katie was still surprised by how Lee communicated with Avery. It was clear from his interactions with her that he felt he'd known Avery for years.

Could it be that Avery was actually much more involved in the company than she let on? She wore long-sleeved shirts with relatively tight cuffs to hide her bracelet, but Katie noticed her attempts weren't all that successful. Every time Avery reached out for her drink, Katie could see a small glint from the silver, usually a few links dangling below the cuff, almost seeming to emphasize the bracelet even more than the three-quarter sleeve fashions that were becoming all the rage.

The ghost of an idea of Avery as a shadow agent for the company, secretly wandering around, infiltrating grassroots groups such as theirs in order to undermine their effectiveness, floated through Katie's mind, but she shook it free. They were only four members of the community, with little to no power of their own. The kind of cloak-and-dagger thoughts Katie was having were more suitable for high-stakes government takeover attempts or thrilling detective novels.

Avery's reaction to her image being on an important page of the Heron Company's internal website was clearly a surprise, but Katie couldn't decide what kind of surprise it was. Had Avery been surprised that her picture was available to Heron employees that way, or was she simply surprised that Lee would make that fact known to the rest of the group? It hadn't escaped Katie's attention that Avery had seemed bothered by Lee's arrival at their table, or that Lee had clearly known who Avery was and felt comfortable enough to speak with her on a first-name basis.

Of course, he had also spoken to Sarah and Ian on a first-name basis, but he had actually spoken with both of them in the past. Maybe it didn't mean anything, after all. Katie was having a hard time these days keeping her thoughts straight. She went back and forth between believing in the girl's sincerity and believing she was playing some kind of elaborate game.

Katie was glad she had decided to go to dessert with Ian after the meeting to bury her suspicions in chocolate cake rather than go home with all these ideas in her mind trying to poison her relationships. At dessert, she and Ian ended up comparing notes about those two moments and agreeing that Avery's reactions seemed strange, but neither could tell whether she was sincerely estranged from her father or playing some elaborate game. Ian tended to side in favor of Avery's sincerity while Katie had a harder time accepting the girl's innocence. She did, however, concede that her own dark experiences with the company and her still fresh grief might be clouding her judgment.

After a fitful night of sleep, Katie sat in front of her mirror, trying to figure out what bothered her so much. She'd known Avery received one of the Phase Two bracelets before they met, but it still bothered her to see it. That wasn't based on anything she felt about Avery, but how she felt about the fact that Ella wasn't wearing it. But Katie wasn't about to allow simple jealousy to stand in the way of their project.

Avery seemed sincere in her unhappiness about meeting with her father, but he was still her father. However estranged they might have become over the years, would Avery still feel she owed him some kind of loyalty? Even if she wasn't colluding with him now, would she be easily swayed over to his side if he asked? And if she were, what would that mean to the rest of them?

Katie decided what was making her feel so uncomfortable was the idea that they had left everything in Avery's hands. If she didn't act, they would likely achieve nothing. Whatever Avery's intentions, they had essentially brought themselves to a dead end.

That was unacceptable. Katie could not allow this project to die simply because the only person who could act right now was the only one who had a bracelet and a motive to go along with the company line. It meant too much to Katie.

With determination, Katie sat down at her computer and pulled up the email Sarah had sent. She spent several hours trying to get some useable details out of the images. Her stomach eventually reminded her that she had other needs, and she was surprised to find it was nearly dinnertime again.

While she sat in the quiet house and ate her dinner, she admitted to herself that if she could spend the whole day trying to track down images, it was time for her to return to work. At first, it had been exhausting just to remember how to get up in the morning and take a shower. It was hard to accept, but she was already starting to move on.

Katie felt a little guilty about that and wondered if that was how a mother was supposed to feel. The sadness was ever-present, but the light was starting to come in. She wondered if she ever would feel happy again. But whether right or wrong, moving on was what she needed to do now.

Having made that decision, Katie returned to thinking about what she had learned through her research.

After becoming frustrated with trying to get clearer images of the papers and finally admitting there just wasn't enough information to read what they said, Katie had turned her attention to trying to identify any of the individuals in the panel. One of the images seemed to have a strong resemblance to the city manager, but he could also be a few other people Katie had found in the area papers. In search of images in local publications to try to find a match, the results found of the city manager's image seemed to reinforce her suspicions.

The possibility of a connection between city management and the private corporation that was suddenly gaining so much power in the community frightened Katie, and she wondered just what they had gotten themselves into.

Her suspicions about Avery flared again, and she struggled to talk herself back down. Part of the problem of living on her own was the opportunity to spend too much time thinking. Just when she thought she was talking herself insane, Katie's thoughts were interrupted by her phone.

"Hey, Katie, got a minute?"

It was Ian, just the person she really needed to talk to. Katie felt a little shiver go down her spine but didn't take time to analyze it.

"Ian. Yes. What's on your mind?"

"I know we talked about Avery's reactions to Lee Park last night, but I was wondering if you were still feeling the same way today."

"Actually, I was thinking about all of that today," Katie admitted. "In fact, I spent most of the day trying to figure out who those people were on Sarah's panel. I don't know whether Avery is truly as in the dark about all this as we are, or if she's a part of the plot, but I do know I'm not comfortable leaving everything in her hands."

Katie could hear Ian laughing on the other end of the line.

"What's so funny?" she demanded, feeling a little miffed that he was laughing at her.

"You," Ian said after a moment. "I knew you wouldn't be able to let it rest, so I spent today trying to talk Lee into sharing that 'Family Tree' he showed Avery with me. I thought maybe if we had some other leads to follow, we'd have an easier time letting Avery do her part of the job."

"So, did he tell you who they are?"

"Not exactly," Ian admitted. Katie could just see the wry grimace he'd make to express his frustration. "He agreed to confirm or deny."

"What does that mean?"

"That means he won't just hand me a list, but if I come to him with a name, he'll tell me whether that person is involved in the funding or top corporate offices of Heron Company."

"How does that help us?"

"Well, we can identify some people involved immediately because of public record," Ian explained. "Those would include people like Reuben Wilkins and Theta Technologies. But companies like Heron will often have silent partners or investors who prefer to remain anonymous, at least as far as the general public is concerned. If we can identify some of those people, we might be able to start figuring out what the overall plan is."

"You mean whether they are actually attempting to restructure our social system?"

"Or at least reinforce their existing status," Ian told her.

"So how do we identify those people?"

"It won't be effective to just start throwing names out. Mr. Park isn't going to have much patience for us going on a random fishing trip. We need to make some strongly educated guesses to limit how often we put Lee at risk."

"I don't understand," Katie admitted. Ian's professional world was entirely new to her, and she was constantly fascinated by the insights he gave her.

"If Lee gives us a name we didn't legitimately come up with on our own, the leak can easily be traced back to him and put him in danger."

"Oh," Katie said. She was starting to understand how this all worked. "Okay, did you have any names to start with yet?"

"No, that's as far as I got," Ian said. "I'll get started on that tomorrow."

"Well, I think you can start with the city manager," Katie said with a certain amount of pride in her voice.

"Really?"

"Yes, I spent some time combing over those photos and trying to find a match on the internet. I think he's the man in the center image Sarah sent."

"Wow, you weren't kidding when you said you have been thinking about this. Nice work, Katie! I'll give Lee a call in the morning and see if this gets us anywhere."

Chapter 23

Avery spent a few days mentally preparing for her promised visit to Theta Technologies. She thought through whether she wanted to make an appointment or not and what she wanted to say. She knew she would likely get flustered while she was there, having not seen her father in years and all, and she figured the more she rehearsed in her mind, the smoother it would likely go.

She decided she would go on Tuesday after class. Businesses might be busy on Monday mornings trying to get caught up on everything that had happened during the weekend. She wasn't sure why she was considering what would be convenient for Reuben since she had rejected him long before, but it might have been because it was simply in her nature to be polite, or maybe it would make Reuben more agreeable if she took his schedule into consideration.

She also thought going in on Tuesday would be better for her, both because it worked well with her schedule and because she would call to make her appointment on Monday. That way, she wouldn't be dropping in unannounced, but at the same time, she wouldn't be giving Reuben much time to work on why she might be requesting a meeting. She'd be able to hit the gym Monday after school, taking some of the tension out of waiting, and it would not bother her too much to take Tuesday off to deal with this Reuben thing.

The only problem with this plan was that she forgot to make the phone call on Monday to make an appointment. She was going to have to show up Tuesday unannounced after all.

When Tuesday arrived, she got ready for the day just as if it were any other day. Her impending meeting with Reuben was on her mind, but she knew she was going there with a job to do, and she was intent on following through. Reuben as a factor in that equation was simply an obstacle that came with the territory as far as Avery was concerned. She did her best to push her feelings aside regarding the meeting and tried instead to focus on simply completing each task of her day.

After classes were over, she headed to Theta headquarters without any hesitation. It was just the next task on her list. It did take some time for her to get to the complex, as it was on the outskirts of town, and she had never driven there before. The complex was extremely large and simply could not be accommodated closer to the city, but she hadn't realized before just how large the company had grown. Once inside the complex's grounds, it took her some effort to figure out where to find Reuben's office.

Avery parked and walked toward the entrance to the main building. Once she entered into an impressive lobby, the security man at the desk looked up and said, "Avery?" He quickly corrected his surprised tone and said, more calmly, "Avery, what can I do for you?"

It disturbed her that this man knew her name without ever having met her before. It was the same with Lee Park from the Heron Company. Why was it that all of the employees of Heron and Theta seemed able to recognize her? Of course, now she knew about the internal website, but it was still creepy. Who paid attention to that kind of stuff? However, she didn't have time just then to concern herself with the details. She had a job to do. In fact, at this moment, she was hopeful it might work to her advantage. Rather than take issue with the guard, she simply replied, "Yes, I would like to see Reuben Wilkins."

"Is he expecting you?" His voice was tight.

"No, he is not, but I would like to see him nevertheless," she replied.

He immediately went into action, "Certainly, Ms. Wilkins…er…I mean Ms. Jensen. I will let him know that you are on your way up. Derek will take you the rest of the way." He said this as he pointed to his partner security guard, simultaneously giving him instructions and telling Avery he would take her.

Derek took the cue and began showing Avery to the boss's office. Avery could tell he was nervous about it and tried to help him relax.

"Bet this is a little weird, me coming here like this, right?"

"It's just that you're unexpected is all," he tried to explain as they walked. "Of course, you're his daughter. I'm sure he'll be glad to see you. Still, he doesn't like to be interrupted."

The guard's nervousness was starting to rub off on Avery as they got closer to Reuben's office. She didn't need the extra help and wondered if maybe she should have put off her trip until after she'd been able to set an appointment after all.

Meanwhile, Derek's partner back at the security desk

was already phoning the boss to warn him of his visitor. "Mr. Wilkins, Avery is on her way up to you."

"Avery?" Reuben's voice came through calmly but with surprise in his tone.

"Yes, Avery. She should be there any moment. Derek is bringing her up."

"Okay, Steve. Thank you," Reuben said and hung up on a relieved guard who no longer feared for his job.

Reaching an ornate set of oak double doors, Derek knocked on one and poked his head in the doorway upon hearing a noise from within. Avery heard him as he spoke into the room beyond "Mr. Wilkins…I am so sorry to disturb you."

Reuben interrupted before Derek could provide more detail, "Send her in."

That is exactly what Derek did.

Avery entered Reuben Wilkins' office for the first time, trying to remember what she knew of this man and deciding he was a total stranger. As she walked into an impressive room decorated with dark woods and heavy furnishings, she saw him. Reuben was standing there behind his desk and next to his large comfortable desk chair, looking like he didn't know what to do any more than she did. Once Avery entered, and the door had been closed behind her, Reuben's arms seemed to spread to his sides of their own volition, as if he thought she might want to rush in for an exuberant reuniting hug, but Avery kept her distance. She wanted it to be clear to him that this visit was just about business. She didn't want Reuben to think this was a personal visit or that she was interested in any form of family reunion. She didn't have the time or energy for that.

"Hello, Avery," Reuben said. "It is so wonderful to see you."

"Hello, Reuben," she said. "I have actually come

here to ask for your help." Better to get right to the point and bypass any personal conversation, she thought.

Reuben dismissed her detached greeting for the time being with a nod. "There will be time to catch up later, I suppose. How are you?"

Avery supposed even in business meetings it was important to spend a few moments getting acquainted. As much as it irritated her, she knew he had the upper hand since she needed something from him, so she tried to engage but as minimally as possible. "Things have been really good, Reuben."

"I have so wanted to see you."

Avery was fuming at this point. She came here to talk business, and he was acting like they'd been Daddy-Daughter all these years. She was having trouble keeping it together. "What is it with all these people knowing my name, Reuben? That's creepy!" she blurted out.

"Avery, honey, you're my daughter. Even though we haven't been in the best of contact over the years, I talk about you with the people I work with. I also needed my employees to know that if you were to ever come by, as you did today, how I expected them to respond."

Avery rolled her eyes. "Not the best of contact?" she said. "That's a very interesting way of putting it."

Reuben shrugged.

She pulled it together and readdressed why she was there in the first place. "About that favor?"

"What is it, Avery?" He took a seat in his chair and motioned that Avery should make herself comfortable as well.

"I have learned that you, or your company or whatever, are financial supporters for the Heron Company."

"Yes?"

"I have been learning about the practices of the Heron Company in their allocation of Phase Two plans and have learned that they are not providing them to applicants equitably. Are you aware of this?"

"I do not question their practices," Reuben answered carefully. "I simply funded what I knew to be a company providing an impressive service, which I am certain will be a good investment….and, you did get a plan, correct?"

"Yes, but that's not the point. I only got a plan because I was trying to get information on Heron."

"Well, I can't imagine what you would need to know to require such drastic measures. Whatever your reasons, I am glad you have a plan."

Avery was frustrated with this discussion. It seemed she was not getting anything she wanted, but she knew she had to press on with her mission to get help from Reuben.

"Is there anything you can do to help pressure Heron to clean up their practices and provide plans in a more equitable manner?" she asked, feeling defeated but wanting to make every effort since she had already come all this way.

For a few moments, Reuben just looked at her. Then, to her surprise, he said, "I am not sure what change I can influence, but if it means so much to you, I will take this concern to them."

"Thank you," she said with an exhausted sigh. "You *can* pressure them, Reuben. I know you can. You provide them with their money."

Reuben grimaced when she called him by his first name, but this was the most contact they had had since she'd been a small child, and he was clearly working to control his own temper. Avery watched his jaw work as he struggled with something and then apparently decided it wasn't important enough to go into at this point. "I'll see what I can do," he said, adopting a businesslike tone. He picked up the phone, obviously connected directly to a secretary somewhere. "Get me Heron," he said. After a moment, he was clearly connected and started talking with the other person on the line. "Tell me more about your candidate selection process. What are the criteria?...Uh huh. I see. How hard would it be to open up enrollment a little?...What if I said I wanted you to?...Really? There must be some room for negotiation?...You know I can't accept that. Clearly, this is going to require more than a phone call. When is your next available opening?...Fine, we'll meet then."

Reuben turned back to a stunned Avery. "This may take some time," he told her. "If you leave your information with the front desk, I will get in touch with you as soon as I have met with them."

"Okay. I will. Thank you," Avery said, genuinely meaning it.

She was fairly certain Reuben already had her contact information. He seemed to have access to everything else, but she found it thoughtful that he requested it and was amazed that he had tried to honor her request right there in front of her.

She walked down to the front desk, thinking perhaps Reuben wasn't quite as bad as she'd made him out to be in her mind. She provided Steve the security guard with her contact information and headed out of the building, feeling extremely content with the progress she had made. She'd gone through a roller coaster of emotions in the past half hour from nervous and afraid to angry to stunned and amazed. Even though the meeting was emotionally draining, she knew it had been worth it.

Chapter 24

Avery was feeling pretty good about herself having successfully navigated the challenging task of confronting her estranged father, both personally and practically. She was happy that in spite of being tentative about helping the group by talking to her father, she had been able to see it through. She was feeling fairly good about how things ended with Reuben, too. She couldn't have expected any more, really. She had been able to meet him, and she avoided personal conversations for the most part, and Reuben had tried to work with Heron for her. So now, she just had to wait to hear from him when he had a chance to talk with them in more detail.

She sent out an email to the group to let them know how the meeting went and what the next steps were.

Hey, team,

I did it. I met with Reuben, and believe it or not, he tried to call while I was standing there in his office. There was some kind of problem, so Reuben said he would talk to them further. I am waiting to hear back from him about their meeting, and then I will get in touch and let you guys know what he says.

Keep your fingers crossed.
Avery

So, Avery waited. It was a week later before she got a message from Reuben.

Avery, I spoke with Heron as you requested, and I have some news. Please give me a call when you have a moment.

Avery's heart was racing. She was really excited, but she was also really nervous. She was trying to imagine what the company had said but hoped, since Reuben provided so much financial backing for Heron, if he requested something, they would oblige.

It was just after five in the evening when she got the message, so she figured it was worth a shot to try to catch Reuben at Theta.

She hadn't bothered to write down his direct number or save it in her phone, so she was limited to calling the front desk receptionist. As soon as the woman answered the phone, Avery introduced herself and announced she would like to speak to Reuben. She knew she would be quickly dismissed if she wasn't careful but hoped everyone else at the company "knew" her as well as Lee claimed. Obviously, Theta wouldn't put through every request to speak to Reuben Wilkins with the number of calls the company must receive.

It was clear, by the receptionist's response, that she understood exactly who Avery was.

She was on hold only a short while before Reuben was connected with her.

"Avery! I assume you got my message?"

"Yes! I'm eager to hear what they had to say."

"Well, before we get into that, I want to make clear that I worked at this extremely hard and even if you are disappointed in the result, I hope you know what it took from me to get to this point."

This had Avery worried but also interested. "What do you mean?" she asked.

"As you heard when you were in my office, this was not something that could be solved through a simple phone call. The executives at Heron have a specific action plan they want to follow in rolling their product out to the public. They were not happy about my request to change the plan."

"So, they do have a plan?" Avery tried to keep the excitement out of her voice. Could it be possible that she would get confirmation for Ian that Heron Company really was trying to change the fabric of their society?

"Every company has a marketing plan, Avery," Reuben said, a trace of exasperation in his voice.

"And that changes who can have access to the product?"

"Frequently."

"Oh. Sooo, what did they say?"

"So, after some negotiations, Heron has agreed, not to an overall change in their policies, I'm afraid, but they have agreed to allow twenty Phase Two plans, free of initial fees, to be awarded by a team of your choosing."

Avery was stunned. She did not see this coming and didn't really know how to react. "Are you joking?"

"Not in the least, Avery," he said. "This took strong negotiations on my part to even reach this agreement. Heron provides a desirable commodity, and they know it is profitable for me, and so negotiations were difficult. They are perfectly content with the way they allocate plans and did not appreciate me stepping in to dictate changes. Not only did I have to pull some strings to get the right people in the room together at short notice, but I also had to throw some weight around to get those people to agree to any form of concession. Even then, it took a lot of negotiation to get this much of an agreement passed. You really should be happy with this, Avery."

Avery didn't know how she felt or even how she should feel. "Thank you, Reuben," she finally said. "I mean, I appreciate your efforts. But what am I supposed to do? I've never picked a committee before, and now they're making me one of them. It isn't right." Avery suddenly felt extremely overwhelmed. She was just a college kid. What did she know about running business panels? She wasn't even sure what she needed to concentrate on first. Before he could say anything else to send her into another tailspin, she decided her best bet was just to get off the phone, let things process, and maybe call Sarah. "Um, I need to go."

"Avery! Wait! It's important!"

"What?" Avery didn't want to deal with anything else, and if he was about to try to get back to family stuff, she was ready to launch into him.

"Before you go…Heron says they need the twenty names within the next two weeks. They will begin advertisements this week with this promotion as a contest. Part of the challenge of the contest will be the short duration. You will need to let me know any details you want them to include in the advertisements."

"You mean they are eager to advertise this?" Avery asked, annoyed that it did not seem as if this compromise was putting Heron out any. Instead, they were turning it into some big PR campaign that Avery was going to have to work for free.

"Believe me, Avery. They did not want to do this, but they're a business and have learned to make an opportunity out of any misfortune, and that is exactly what they are trying to do here. Nevertheless, they had to make concessions, and you should be proud of that."

"I guess. It's hard to see it that way right now," Avery said letting a bit of emotion seep through the guarded front she had set out for her interactions with Reuben. "All right, I'll see what kind of details I can come up with."

"Don't forget, you'll need your panel ready to make decisions quickly once the applications have been submitted."

"Wait, they want everything, the advertising, collecting the applications, and decisions made all within two weeks?" It was impossible. There was no way she could both learn everything she needed to know and get the project completed within such a short time.

Then she realized, that was exactly the point. The company was creating such impossible rules so that the contest would fail and all the blame would fall on Avery's head instead of Heron. Heron would come out of it looking like the hero that had tried to create a humanitarian program. If it failed under her leadership, they could then use the failure as ammunition to ward off any future efforts. If Avery refused the challenge, then she'd be admitting defeat just as much as if she tried and failed.

Her anger was growing by the second as Reuben was lecturing her in the background, something about how he'd really put his neck out for her and how difficult it could be to work with large companies such as Heron Company, or whatever.

Her only burning question at the moment was whether he was a part of this grand scheme to force her failure, or if he really was as powerless over the company as he was claiming. She decided it really wouldn't pay to make him angry with her at the moment by accusing him of working against her. Instead, she'd try feeling him out a bit more.

"Reuben, you know that's impossible. No one can start and end a contest this important in just two weeks!"

The exasperated sigh from the other end of the call let Avery know she was getting to him, but she couldn't be sure if it was her continued use of his first name or her continued resistance to the plan.

"I know, but I bet, once you think on it, you will see this is progress," he finally said. "You can take a day or two to think about it but not too long."

"Maybe you should tell me about this timeline they seem to think we can follow."

"They need details for the advertisements by Thursday morning so designers can get them inserted and running in time for weekend viewing. Airing will begin Friday morning, applicants will have until Monday evening to get their forms submitted. That will then give your team a few days to make your decisions. The names of the twenty people to receive free plans will need to be submitted to Heron no later than eight o'clock Friday morning."

She decided to confront him head-on. "That kind of schedule is designed to make me fail."

"Those were the best terms I could get. Are you saying you refuse?"

For the first time, Avery wished she knew this man a little better. She couldn't tell from his tone whether he was admitting he was part of putting up the roadblocks or daring her to rise to the challenge. Either she failed by trying or failed by not trying. At least if she tried, there was a slight chance she might win.

"How big does the panel need to be?"

"Heron left that to your discretion."

Avery wasn't sure if it was right to put this decision

on the backs of so few people as her four-person investigation group, but at least they would give her a place to start. They really didn't have much of a choice at this point.

"I guess I don't have much choice," she said. "I'm not going to let this opportunity pass by just because they thought they could make me fail."

"Good."

Reuben sounded satisfied, and again she wondered if somehow she had managed to jump through one of his hoops. She hated feeling like someone else's tool, but she just couldn't figure out where he stood.

"Get back to me about any information you think Heron might need to include in their advertisements for this."

"Okay. Thank you," Avery said. "I will. Talk to you soon."

After getting off the phone with Reuben, Avery sat and made some notes about what they'd talked about, but before she was ready to contact the rest of the group, she had to spend a bit of time sorting through her feelings about Reuben. Her head was spinning from the many possibilities that came to light during her phone conversation.

She was used to being skeptical of companies and their motives. It was something of a game she'd played with her mother all through high school and one of the reasons she'd signed up for the Science and Society class in the first place. She was interested in learning more about the dynamics of the commercial-social interactions. And as much as she'd been trying to investigate Heron, she admitted she'd also been caught up in its science and the hype. Now she had family dynamics entering into it, too. Even when Reuben behaved himself and kept personal connections out of his side of the conversation, she couldn't help but suspect deeper personal connections behind his motives. She wondered what kind of price she might need to pay for his help later.

Chapter 25

The email she received from Avery that morning sounded panicked from the subject line. Checking the time stamp, Katie saw that it was dated last night around ten o'clock, and the subject line simply read: *We NEED to talk!*

Katie read the rest of the message:

Hey, guys,

I got a response back from Reuben, and rather than outline it here, I think it would be better if we met in person again, as soon as possible. I am going to suggest we meet at Brio on Wednesday at 6:00 P.M. I hope everyone can make it, but either way, I think we should go ahead with the meeting, because I need to get back to Heron on something by Thursday morning.

See you Wednesday, I hope.

Avery

When Wednesday came, Katie found herself running uncharacteristically late. She hated being late to anything but allowed herself to relax a little when she remembered

Sarah's joking comment about "Avery time" and realized Avery would probably be running late for the meeting anyway. Just to be on the safe side, though, she decided to call Ian so he could make excuses for her.

"Ian, please let everyone know I'm on my way," Katie huffed into the phone as she tried to balance her purse and her work bag while keeping the phone pinned between her shoulder and ear.

She heard a laugh coming from the other end.

"Can't do it, ma'am," Ian's soft voice drifted over her. She stopped moving for a moment to take in his calming energy. "I'm running a bit late myself. Just leaving the office now."

Katie giggled a little. It was kind of funny that two people who prided themselves on being on time were both running late on the same night. What were the odds of that?

"Well, you'll still be at the cafe before I am."

"Don't worry," Ian told her. "Remember what Sarah said, Avery's always late."

"Even though she set the meeting?"

"I admit I'm interested to hear what she has to say. It sounded pretty urgent in her email."

"Yes, it did. I'll be there as soon as I can."

"Drive safely," Ian told her.

She hung up feeling less flustered than when she'd called. She told herself it was just because she wouldn't be causing people stress wondering if she was coming. She wasn't ready to consider whether she wanted to feel something about Ian or any other human being yet.

When Katie arrived at the Brio, she waited to be assisted by a hostess at the front door. As the hostess helped the customers in front of Katie, the light happened to fall on a gold foil sticker that had been added to the front window featuring the P2 logo in its center. Katie was surprised to see it here, knowing that sticker meant the business catered to the Phase Two policy holders and wondered what that might mean for regular customers such as herself. She found out as the hostess responded to whatever the customers in front of Katie had said.

"I am afraid that the restaurant is only seating customers with reservations and our preferred customers at this time."

Katie was just as surprised as the people in front of her and listened as the man tried to argue he'd been coming to the restaurant for years and never needed a reservation before, but the hostess was unmoved. As the customers made their way back out past Katie, she wondered if she would have trouble too.

"Hello, may I help you?" the hostess looked at her with a bland, expectant look on her face.

"I'm supposed to meet three friends here at six o'clock," Katie said, feeling her voice break.

"Oh, yes, you'll be with Ms. Jensen's party. Right this way, please." The hostess led Katie through the restaurant and out to the patio where Katie was relieved to see Avery, Sarah, and Ian already gathered around one of the few occupied tables.

As they all got settled, Katie mentioned how surprised she was to find the patio so empty at this hour and the strange encounter she'd witnessed at the door between the hostess and the other customers. "With all these open seats back here, you'd think they'd be happy for the business," she finished.

"I'm surprised they let us in," Sarah said.

"Yes, well it was Avery who arrived first, wasn't it?" Ian said with a pointed look toward Avery's wrist.

Katie's eyes followed his to see that Avery once again wore a long-sleeved shirt that was carefully covering the sparkling silver bracelet everyone knew hid inside. Looking up, Katie could see Avery's face was flushed.

"I saw the sign when I got here, and the hostess told me about their new policy. It was already too late to change the location on everyone, and I didn't want anyone to feel bad about this."

"It's all right, Avery. You didn't make the rules," Sarah said, reaching out to pat her friend's hand.

"I really didn't want to give this restaurant our business if that's the way they were going to be, but I didn't know what else to do. I was hoping to just play it off cool this time and then suggest a different restaurant from now on."

Katie was touched that Avery put so much thought into how the rest of them would feel upon arriving at the restaurant. She had to admit, she hadn't felt good about the people being turned away at the door and had been a little relieved to realize that she wouldn't be one of them. She couldn't quite bring herself to thank Avery for it out loud, but she made a mental note to give her more of the benefit of the doubt whenever she was unsure of her intentions in the future.

With the sensation of the restaurant's drastic change in policies fully discussed, Ian turned the conversation back to the reason for Avery's urgent message with a question.

After thanking everyone for dropping everything to come meet with her, Avery told the group what Reuben had told her about Heron's offer. When she told them they would need to select twenty people who would be granted Phase Two plans, within two weeks, Katie gasped. Looking around at everyone else's reactions, it seemed Sarah was just as surprised as she was, but Ian seemed to have been expecting something like this.

"We cannot do this!" Sarah said. "We'll be just like Heron if we give plans to some and not to others who also need it. We'll just be another panel like they have at their headquarters, just another small group deciding who lives and who does not."

"But we have to try," Katie pleaded. "At least it's twenty more people who have a chance. It's a start. We can't pass it up."

"I am sure Heron intended it to be impossible and to challenge our sense of ethics," Ian said. "The way I see it, we're damned if we do, damned if we don't."

"I'm sure you see why I thought we had to meet. I have to tell Heron what we need for their advertisements, but I am not even sure we should be doing this at all," Avery said. "I only have until tomorrow to get them the details. I told Reuben we would take the offer because he was pressuring me, but I wanted to get your opinions. We can still back out by just not giving them details if you don't think we should do this."

The women continued to discuss around and around, talking about the pros and cons of going ahead as well as turning down the offer. As they talked out their thoughts and ideas, it became clear that there were no clear decisions among them. Sarah's gut feeling was that it was a bad idea that opened them up to an unknown number of ethical problems and didn't really address the problem they had with the company.

Katie felt an obligation to do whatever she could to get plans into the hands of the people who needed them but couldn't afford them, and Avery was still unsure as to what the appropriate course of action should be. The only one who hadn't contributed much to the conversation so far was Ian, who had characteristically sat back and listened to the others talk.

"What do you think we should do?" Avery asked him, realizing he had not yet taken a strong stand in either direction.

"Well, I'm not sure if there is a right thing here, but I don't know if I would feel comfortable knowing that twenty people could have received a Plan but didn't simply because we were a little uneasy about it. Also, this is a form of compromise from Heron, no matter what their intentions were in making it so difficult for us. They could have said 'piss off,' but they offered something. I think, if we want any kind of change to occur, we have to accept that, initially, the changes may not be exactly as we pictured. This, at least, would give us a foot in the door, and we may be able to leverage that into more concessions in the future, especially if we manage to pull this off."

Avery and Katie were nodding. He made a convincing case, but Sarah reiterated her concern. "I think we're making a mistake if we go ahead with this, but if that's what the rest of you think is best, I'll put my reservations aside, help out where I can, and hope for the best."

"So, it's a go?" Avery asked tentatively.

The group agreed.

"Well, I know this is a lot, but I have to tell Heron what we need in the advertisement," Avery said.

"I guess, we need them to fill out some kind of application," Katie said.

"All right." Avery pulled out a notebook she had packed just for this purpose. "What should it include?"

The group started listing things while Avery worked to jot them down.

"Name, of course."

"Contact info."

"Statement of why they need a plan?"

"What about if they have applied for a plan before?" Katie asked.

"Why would that matter?"

"Well, if they applied for a plan in the past and were refused, it's not very likely they'll be reassessed," Katie pointed out, feeling a twinge of pain deep in her heart that Ella would never get a second chance.

"Should we have them send in their income statements like Heron does?" Sarah asked.

Katie was offended. "Why would we want to do that?"

Sarah had been the one arguing that it felt like they were being asked to become too much like the Heron panels. It seemed completely wrong for her to now suggest they do the same thing.

"We shouldn't be awarding these plans to people who could afford them on their own and are just looking for a free hand out." The look on Sarah's face was intense and Katie could tell that she felt the same sense of injustice Katie had been feeling only moments before. She was surprised by how often she had to remind herself that these people felt much the same way she did about how this company was operating.

"Anything else?" Avery asked, breaking up the moment of tension.

The group looked around at one another to confirm that no one had any other additions.

"All right. I will send these to Reuben," Avery said, with a bit of trepidation in her voice about what they were getting into. "Thanks for meeting, everyone. I will let you know what I hear. Hopefully, we are doing the right thing, but we certainly know that, no matter what, we are putting forth our best effort for change, and we should be proud of that."

Katie looked around at the faces at the table and realized everyone was feeling some trepidation about this step and whether it was the right thing to do. It was a heavy responsibility, actually placing the right of life and death into their hands. But who really ever should have that kind of responsibility? At least they were in a position to try to make the decision more equitable.

Chapter 26

It had been a few days since the group met and Avery told Reuben of the group's needs for an online application. He'd required her to create her own form to send in and then forwarded it over to Heron on her behalf. He claimed if the form was already made, Heron would not have the excuse of lacking time to design it, but again Avery wondered if he wasn't just getting excited about having her under his control and what his ultimate motive might be. Reuben had assured Avery that Heron would be in contact when there was pertinent information available.

In the morning, Avery's phone buzzed.

Turn on Channel Three. Quick!

It was a text message from Sarah. Avery complied.

When her TV came to life, she could see it was a Heron commercial. She had missed the start, but what she did hear was "…go to our website for your chance to have time—time you've always wanted—for *no* initial fee. This is a chance of a lifetime, but it's only available for a limited time."

Avery also saw, during the course of the ad, a due date for the application printed at the bottom of the screen. At the completion of the ad, Avery did two things. She went to her computer, and she called Sarah. As she logged on, she said to Sarah, "Thanks for the heads up. Have you seen the site yet?"

"Not yet. I am going there right now."

"Me, too," Avery said.

As the two looked over the site together, they pointed out different things to one another that they noticed, such as the large countdown timer indicating how much time people had to get their applications in before the opportunity was gone.

"I can't believe how they are spinning this," Sarah said. "It's like they're doing something good for those in financial need out of the kindness of their hearts, not because a reporter and the daughter of one of their big financial backers think they should. I'd much prefer it was clear their hands were tied, and they're only doing this kicking and screaming because someone is forcing them."

"Ian called it the other day. This is a smart company, and they know how to make lemonade out of lemons. Kind of frustrating."

"Have you looked at the form?" Sarah asked.

"No. I'll go there now," Avery answered. "Looks basically like they got what we requested. Do you see anything missing?"

"No. I don't think so. Are you getting these applications when they're filled out or are they holding them to deliver all at once? They are due on Monday! Did you see that?" Sarah said, highlighting the short timeline.

"Right! That timeline is short. I didn't even think

about asking when we'll receive the applications, but Reuben did tell me we'd have until Friday morning to choose our winners. That still doesn't feel like much time, but it does match up with the two-week deadline I was given to get them the names. I haven't heard anything from Reuben yet, but when I do, I'll be sure to ask him about the applications. I'm sure he will be in touch soon."

"Well, it is going to be interesting. I'm just going to have to keep telling myself that while Heron is using this to shamelessly promote themselves as a giving and caring company, when we know full well that they are anything but, we're still going to be able to get twenty people a plan. I hope I can find solace in that."

"I hear you. It's a tough one. Let's just remember Heron is being pressured to make a change they didn't want to, and that's a good thing in my book. It's a step in the right direction." Avery said, and then she followed up with, "I hope."

"All right, girl. Let me know when you hear from Reuben, or Heron, or whatever."

"Will do. Have a good day. Thanks for the heads up on the advertisement. I am glad we saw it and checked out the website, so we know more about what's going on."

Avery spent a jumpy weekend waiting for a call to let her know what was going on with the applications for the contest. She wondered if there were thousands or just a few coming in so she'd be able to prepare for the final selection process. However, the call didn't come until Monday morning. With her deadline just days away and the countdown clock on the contest website down to single digit hours, she was anxious to find out how many applications they would be expected to review and when they would be receiving them.

"Avery? It's your father," Reuben said.

His classification of himself still made Avery uncomfortable. Not only had she always considered Marshall Jensen her father, but now she was still unclear as to Reuben's underlying motivations in helping her. She wondered if he was trying to get on her good side in order to demand something bigger of her later. She decided this was not the time for a confrontation, though, and forced herself to let it go in spite of her jangled nerves.

"Hi. I've been expecting your call," she replied.

"Yes. I am sorry I haven't gotten to you until now. I have been waiting for Heron to provide me with what I needed to pass on to you."

"So, do you have it now?" Avery asked.

"Yes. I have some information for you on how to access the completed applications people have been filling out. Do you have a pen handy?"

"I'll grab something. Hang on a second."

Avery grabbed a pen and paper quickly and returned to the phone where Reuben provided her with an administrator web address, as well as log in and password where she could access the applications.

"Got it," Avery said after carefully copying down the information and reciting it back to Reuben for confirmation of its accuracy. At the same time, she was typing the information into her browser to make sure the links actually worked. She barely had a chance to verify that she actually did have access to the applications before Reuben started talking again. She felt her eyes widen at the four-digit number already on screen.

"Okay so, Avery," Reuben instructed. "The site will accept applications until four fifty-nine p.m., when it will automatically post that the deadline has passed and will no longer accept further submissions. You have access now, so you can start viewing them any time, but be aware applications will still be coming in until then."

"I understand," Avery told him and wondered how she could ever pull this off.

Reuben's tone became deeper and lost any trace of humor it might have had as he started to speak again. "You will receive an email from Heron just after the site closes the application submissions, and you must reply to that email with the twenty names and copies of their application forms by Friday at seven fifty-nine a.m."

"It is still ridiculous that they are giving us barely any time!" Avery said.

"I understand, but those are Heron's expectations, and I expect you will comply, not only because you would not want to toss away this opportunity for people because of carelessness on your part, but additionally, you asked me to stick my neck out for you on this, and I was happy to do it, but I cannot afford for my relationship with Heron to be damaged in some way due to any missteps on compliance with their requests. Do you understand?"

Again, Avery felt a twinge of defiance rise up in her as he took on this parental tone with her, but she managed to put the image of twenty faceless people standing in front of her, all with Phase Two bracelets gleaming on their wrists because of her.

"Yes. I do really appreciate your help with all of this, Reuben. I won't let you down. We will have the names sent off prior to the deadline. I promise," Avery said. If he was sincere in all that he had told her, Reuben was now in a precarious position with Heron because of her request. As willing as he had been to help her, he really didn't know her any more than she knew him and that, of course, would make him nervous.

"Thank you."

Despite recognizing Reuben's position and the possibility that he was nervous about this deal too, Avery couldn't resist asking, "Just out of curiosity, what would happen if we did miss the deadline?"

"Don't go there," Reuben said. "I honestly don't know, Avery, but I don't care to find out. Please."

"I know. I know. I was just curious."

"Don't be. I know you've got this. Good luck."

As soon as she got off the phone with Reuben, she immediately started drafting a message to the group.

Hi, team,

I just spoke to Reuben (finally!) and now have access to the online submissions. The site is set to automatically refuse any applications submitted after 4:59 P.M., but it will continue to receive them up until then. There are already more than 5,000 applications submitted! I've copied the access information below so each of us can start looking through. I am hoping we can meet at Ian's office tomorrow morning since we all need to have access to a computer. Also, we may need to spend a fair amount of time discussing and making our decision, and I am not sure Brio is the best spot for that. Ian, is this all right? Can we meet outside your office in the morning?

I am also hoping that everyone can think about how we should make our decision. With all of these submitted applications, I am hoping we can come up with a plan we all can live with.

See you soon,
Avery

Avery was glad when she sent the email that she could easily justify wanting to meet at a location other than Brio. She hadn't been looking forward to dredging that whole conversation up again, at least not right now when they needed to be focused. It was easy to suggest Ian's office since it was just down the street from the Brio, and everyone knew where it was. It also had that nice big conference room where they could all work. But, too late, she wondered if Ian would be able to use it during a weekday.

Throughout the remainder of the day, Avery used random free moments to check on the status of the website. The number of applications kept growing, and she wondered how they would ever be able to weed that number down to just twenty. When she had the extra time, she read through some of them. Parents with children like Ella, people who had high-risk careers such as military personnel, people who had worked sixty to eighty hours a week their whole lives hoping for some extra years to spend with family. Avery didn't always have a chance to read all the details on the applications, but each one had a desperate story to tell.

She was beginning to have some appreciation for the dilemma Heron Company itself faced. Too many applications coming in from all over, all of them with good reasons for wanting a plan, most without the finances to be able to cover the exorbitant fee. Just how was it possible for a group of humans, any group of humans, to make this kind of decision? And yet, there was only so much business that the company could handle, so the decision had to be made.

Avery was intimidated about the task the group had ahead of them. She was overwhelmed, both by the sheer number of applications submitted and the gargantuan task of selecting the twenty lucky people to get a plan from this enormous pool.

The weight of the responsibility afforded to them with this selection was still heavy on Avery's mind as she tried to sort through the documents again that evening, grateful that the total number of applications had not exceeded 10,000 at least.

Chapter 27

By eight o'clock that night, Avery was beginning to get concerned again that she had yet to hear from Ian. Everyone in the group was aware that the timeline was short and had been keeping fairly close tabs on each other, but now when she actually had news, no one seemed to be around. She started to incessantly check her email for any response from her team. Finally, she heard from Ian.

> *Avery and team,*
> *Sorry I haven't responded until now. Breaking news items had me out in the field all day. It sounds great to meet at my office in the morning. There is a staff meeting at 8, but it is usually only 30 minutes or so. I can have the conference room set up for us by 9 A.M. I am hoping that will work for everyone.*
> *See you tomorrow!*
> *Ian*

Avery was relieved to hear from Ian, and she immediately texted Sarah.

You coming tomorrow? I hope so.

Yeah. I just got Ian's email. Sorry, I was kind of waiting until we heard from him before I said anything. I'm a little intimidated, but I'm sure we can do it, Sarah texted back.

I'm glad you will be there. I am nervous, too, but I know we can do this. We worked hard for this, and it will feel great to see it through.

You're right. See you tomorrow.

See you.

Avery was glad that at least three of them would be there. She was certain Ian would make sure Katie was there. Avery didn't feel comfortable pressing the still-grieving mother. For the rest of the night, Avery's emotions went bouncing around a number of concerns. How would they deal with the weight of their decision? How would they handle all those applications? Would everyone be able to get to the meeting in the morning? Even though she was still overwhelmed, she was comforted in knowing she had the support and backup of Ian, Sarah, and Katie.

She was ready to meet with them and complete this mission. That was not to say that once the twenty names were selected Avery felt their job was done, but it would feel good to have evidence the group had made some progress.

Avery was uncharacteristically prompt in her arrival at the Wencler Building the next morning. Despite her on-time arrival, Sarah and Katie were already there and chatting nervously as they waited for the elevator. They seemed pleasantly surprised when she arrived just before the doors opened.

They didn't talk much on the elevator ride up, all of them feeling nervous about the task ahead of them, but when the doors opened, Avery was able to confidently lead them to the conference room where she and Ian had met once before.

He had clearly gone to some lengths to set the room up for them.

The room contained the expected large table with chairs around it, and Ian had four laptops as well as pads of paper and pens set up near each other at one end. On the other end of the table, were beverages along with trail mix, bagels and cream cheese, muffins, and scones.

When the group saw the room, they each commented simultaneously how incredible it was and how thoughtful it was for him to take the time to set this up.

Ian looked around at each of them when he responded but concluded as he was looking at Katie and gave her a smile when he said, "It was no problem at all. I just thought we might as well be comfortable if we're going to be here together for a while."

"Thank you, Ian," Katie said.

"Nicely done, Mr. Callahan!" Avery said, certainly knowing this would make the day easier but also picking up on the fact that this was likely more for Katie than for anyone else. Either way, it was thoughtful and above and beyond what Avery expected. It certainly brightened the mood and got the group started on a positive note.

"The paper has also agreed to allow us use of the room tomorrow if we need it and will pick up the tab for our lunches."

"What do they want in return?" Katie asked.

"Nothing." Ian shrugged. "They're paying me back a favor I did for them a long time ago."

Katie and Ian stared at each other for a moment until Sarah broke things up.

"Sooo?" she said, directing her questioning toward Avery. "What do we do now?"

"I am not exactly sure where to begin," she said. "I know I asked you all to think of how we should make this decision, so maybe we should compare notes about how we should limit our decisions."

"Honestly, I haven't had much chance to look over the applications," Katie said. "I spent most of my day yesterday working to get the time off for this project."

"I was in the field yesterday, I need a bit of time to look over things, too," Ian admitted.

It was understood that the team would need to take the start of the meeting to review the applications on their own prior to their discussion.

Initially, there were a few comments as everyone settled into the reading. Avery heard comments like, "What? Really, we have this many applications?" and "Oh, my gosh!" But eventually things settled down, and the four of them flipped through applications on their own, sometimes jotting down notes as they read.

It was quiet for several hours, each of them getting up for more food or for restroom breaks randomly as they read. It was early afternoon when sniffling could be heard coming from Katie. Sarah broke the silence when she asked, "Katie? Are you all right?"

The rest of the group looked up and stopped what they were doing when they realized Katie was upset. They waited for her response to Sarah.

Katie collected herself for a moment, and Ian handed her a box of tissue. "I was just reading this application from a mom asking for a plan for her daughter, and it reminded me of Ella," she said. "I mean, it is not like I've forgotten her, of course. She is always on my mind. But recently I found that I was distracted enough to do a few things, like work with all of you, and then, just reading this right now brought all of those emotions, which have been there the whole time, but were just pushed back a bit, to the front." She paused for a moment then said, "I'm sorry. I'm probably not even making any sense."

Sarah quickly said, "Katie, you have nothing to apologize for. I am sure this is very difficult for you, but we're glad you're here, and if there's anything we can do for you, let us know."

Ian and Avery were nodding in agreement with Sarah.

"Thank you. I'm okay. I guess I just needed a cry," Katie said and let out a choked laugh as she finished her statement. "Maybe, I'll just go wash my face, and when I get back, we can talk about how to do this."

"Are you sure?" Avery said, wondering if she really wanted to continue.

"Yes. I'm sure. I need to do this," Katie said.

"Take whatever time you need," Ian told her.

After only a few minutes, Katie returned looking more refreshed. Her eyes were red, but she had collected herself and looked ready to take on the challenge.

Once she sat down, Avery said, "So, does anyone have any ideas on how the twenty people should be selected?"

There was silence when, finally, Sarah said, "As you all know, I have been concerned about this deal with Heron, and I really think that we—especially now that I see how many applications there are from people, deserving people, who want a plan—that we have to just pick them at random. I mean, who are we to say who deserves it and who doesn't? Isn't that our problem with Heron? That they're doing that? If we pick and choose, we'll be doing the same thing as they are."

"But some of these people haven't even tried to get a plan from Heron yet," Katie said. "I just wouldn't feel right unless we picked people who were denied a plan and who were the most in need financially and situation-ally."

Avery saw that that while Sarah disagreed strongly, she also recognized that Katie was very emotional and passionate about her view. Avery could tell that Sarah was making a sincere effort to be sensitive while voicing her reservations.

"I get what you're saying, but I just don't see how we can determine who is most deserving. I don't feel qualified to say 'you deserve this' and 'you don't.'"

"I guess I don't feel that I would be saying to anyone 'you don't deserve this,' but rather, that I did my best to pick the people I felt needed it the most. I don't think I am making claims about anybody except to say, 'I think these twenty people need a plan.'"

Avery could sense this discussion was not going to get resolved and might even escalate. Unfortunately, she wasn't quite ready to jump in on one side or another. Because she'd been the one to get this deal pushed through, though, she felt it was her responsibility to try to resolve this, not only to keep the peace but because they needed a decision very soon.

"How would you feel about dividing up the twenty names so that we each had five, and then we could pick our five. However, we felt best?"

Avery was pretty happy with this idea and was hoping it would be well received by the group. Ian was the first to respond.

"Avery, that seems like a great idea." He turned to Katie and asked, "Do you think you can live with that?"

"Yes. I think so. It certainly seems fair, although I don't know how I'm ever going to choose just five out of all those thousands of applications."

"Great. How about you?" Ian asked Sarah.

"Yes, as long as I don't have to decide who is deserving and who isn't," Sarah said.

The group could have done without Sarah's last comment, but they let it go, knowing they were coming to a compromise that they all agreed on.

"Perfect," Avery said. "I know we all have other responsibilities we need to take care of, too. This way, we can go home, shower, eat a meal, and make our decisions at home. I just need everyone to email me his or her names by Thursday night. Is that all right?"

They all agreed.

They packed up and helped Ian shut things down in the conference room since regular office hours were now closed, and everyone else had gone home for the day. As they were walking out, Ian and Katie were walking together in front of both Avery and Sarah. They looked at the couple in front of them and at each other significantly, asking each other without words if something was happening there. Then Ian leaned down to Katie and Avery heard him tell her, "You can have my five people if you want."

"You don't have to do that," Katie said.

"I want to," Ian told her.

"Well, thank you, Ian. I will choose them carefully."

"I know you will."

Avery wasn't sure how she felt about that, but she decided not to make an issue of it for now.

The group parted ways, and Avery went home to take a shower before sitting down to choose her people. There was an email from Ian letting her know that he'd given his names to Katie. Obviously, he hadn't been aware she and Sarah could hear him. However, it got Avery thinking about it again. Now Katie would be selecting ten names by reading applications and carefully selecting those she felt would benefit most, and Sarah would be picking five names randomly through whatever method she came up with. And then there were her five names. She thought for only a brief moment before she started a text to Sarah.

Ian has given his selections to Katie, so to keep our selections even, I have decided I want to give my selections to you. Cool?

If you say so, but I'm just picking them randomly. You cool with that?

Yup. Send me the names when you have 'em.

K.

Avery was pretty happy with how things ended up. Now she just had to wait for the names.

Sarah sent Avery her ten names by early the next day, but Katie's names were not there by Thursday evening. Avery got a hurried message from Katie that she was working on it but then sat nervously at her computer waiting for the follow-up message. Avery wondered if she should send the first group of names anyway, just in case, but she was worried Heron would take that as her final answer. She was jolted awake at two a.m. and checked her email in a panic. Finally, the names from Katie were there. She was relieved and copied the names from each of the emails and pasted them into the reply to Heron's request as she'd been instructed. She looked over the email one last time and hit send. Even though she was only half awake, she could feel the intensity of the situation. She was relieved to have sent the names on to Heron so they could uphold their end of the deal, but until that time, there was no way for her to breathe easily. Even then, she knew this was only the beginning of the fight.

Chapter 28

Katie felt a calmness now that the ball was in Heron's court. She thought it might be unsettling since she didn't think highly of the company, but instead she was somewhat at ease knowing that Heron had to compromise. She was also feeling empowered by the work they had done. She felt vibrant and refreshed and was ready to soak up what they had accomplished, but also ready to press on. It was good to start feeling a little more alive again.

She hadn't been sure it would be possible after losing Ella. She hoped the team felt positive about their work, too. She knew that she would soon find out, since the group had been invited to Heron headquarters to be present as the culled twenty got their bracelets. This opportunity from Heron made it so Katie hated them a little bit less. It would never make up for losing Ella, but she would be able to find some gratification in seeing others gain new assurance of life.

The group was set to attend the ceremony in just a few days at Heron headquarters at five p.m. Avery sent word to the group that Heron had contacted her:

Hey, gang,
Can you believe it? Less than 48 hours until we witness firsthand the fruits of our labor.
Heron just let me know that they will be sending a car for us to my place. Can you all be here at 4?
Looking forward to seeing you!
Avery

Ian responded positively to Avery's email, so Katie decided to put her own reservations to the side. Still, she felt it necessary to double check. There were things about Heron that were just a bit too difficult to forget.

I'll be there. Sounds great about the car, but are you absolutely sure Heron understands I will be attending, and they said it was OK? she wrote to Avery.

Rather than just brushing her concerns aside, the time it took for Avery to respond assured Katie that she had actually double-checked with her contact at Heron.

I reminded them of their poor treatment of you in the past and asked for written confirmation that you were invited to attend. Attached is the confirmation they provided. I'm so sorry you had such a bad experience, Avery wrote back.

Sarah's response, copied to the full group, highlighted her disapproval of taking gifts like this car ride from Heron.

Avery,
Thanks for the update. As I am sure you know, I don't think it is a good idea, or in keeping with our position on Heron, to accept this car ride from them. I think it

makes our position against them less overt. It is already a stretch for me to attend this ceremony. I hope you understand.

Sarah

Katie decided she agreed more with Avery on the issue. It would be fun to have a glamorous night out filled with so much happiness. She could use the positive atmosphere. She hoped Sarah would have a change of heart, but she would just have to wait and see.

The day of the ceremony arrived. She'd taken half the day off to give her a chance to prepare and took extra care getting ready. She was pleased with the results when Ian stopped by to pick her up, his eyes lighting up at seeing her. She thought he also looked very polished in his suit and tie, quite different from his everyday attire. With very little delay, they headed off to Avery's.

"Wow! You guys look amazing!" Avery said when she opened the door. "Come in! Have a seat."

Katie asked, "Is Sarah coming?"

"I think she is going to meet us there," Avery replied, obviously disappointed that her friend hadn't arrived.

Katie chose not to press further.

The three caught up while they waited for the car to arrive. They also speculated about the ceremony and gave themselves a pat on the back for their accomplishment.

Soon, there was a knock at the door. Anticipating that it was the driver, they all stood up and headed towards the door. Avery picked up her purse and opened the door.

It was Sarah.

Avery shrieked and gave Sarah a huge hug. "Thank you!" Everyone laughed, and Sarah commented on how amazing everyone looked. Before they had a chance to settle back in, there was another knock at the door.

Since, surely, this could only be the driver, they all got up once again and headed toward the door.

When they arrived at Heron, they were surprised to see hordes of reporters at the entrance.

Instinctively, they each looked at Ian even though they knew he would have most certainly discussed something like a grand press conference.

When he saw their expressions, he retorted, "No way. I didn't have anything to do with this."

The car door opened with Malia standing just outside. She welcomed each of them as they exited the car then led them past the reporters, through the frosted glass doors, and into the lobby.

The lobby was surprisingly calm and empty, considering the hubbub just outside, and the group let out a collective sigh as the sliding doors closed. Malia said, "I am so glad you all could be here for this historic day."

"Thank you for having us," Avery replied.

"Well, shall we?" Malia said, suggesting they should head to a different location.

They followed as Malia led them through the lobby to a room she opened with her key card. All five of them entered to see a table behind which sat four individuals. In front of each of them were five boxes stacked one on top of the other.

There were also several other individuals in the room. A couple of them looked like reporters.

Avery whispered to the group that she recognized her template specialist Warren, and they all recognized Lee Park among a group of stiff-postured Heron employees. Neither Lee nor Warren acknowledged any previous encounters with any members of their group.

Malia directed Avery, Sarah, Katie, and Ian to stand on the opposite side of the room from the Heron employees, and then she addressed the whole room. "Thank you so much to all of you who have made today possible. Heron is honored and delighted to be providing twenty persons in need a Phase Two Plan free of any initial fee. This exemplifies the nature of this company—designing the future but keeping our hearts in the present."

Katie was momentarily getting swept up in the emotion of Malia's speech when Ian shifted slightly on his feet, slightly bumping her and bringing her back to reality. *It is not in Heron's nature to be kind. Who do they think they are kidding?* Katie thought. *They sure do know how to take advantage of a situation.*

She was annoyed that they were portraying themselves in such a positive light, and she knew if she was bothered, the others must also be furious. She tried to remind herself they were helping people, and despite how Heron was spinning it now, they had forced Heron's hand into this.

After Malia's plug for Heron, the door opened, and in walked a line of people, one after another—twenty of them. They looked nervous but also excited, as they should. They walked in and lined up in a single row in front of the table behind which sat the four individuals and the stacks of boxes. The two reporters were ferociously snapping photos when the man sitting behind the table on the far end began to speak.

"Ms. Julie Sanders," he said in a manner similar to what you would expect if someone were announcing a winner of an award.

After he said her name, the first person in the line of twenty stepped forward, and the man who had announced her name took the top box from his stack of five and set it on the table. He opened it slowly.

Avery clenched Sarah's hand, and Katie grabbed Ian's in anticipation.

Ms. Julie Sanders approached the table, and the man took a bracelet out of the box and said, "Ms. Julie Sanders, I present to you your Phase Two bracelet."

She immediately started to cry and held out her wrist as the bracelet was attached and the connecting link was formed with the linkage tool that only Avery had seen before. When the snap of the tool was made, Avery squeezed Sarah's hand, expressing her excitement and acknowledging their contribution to the moment.

As Julie walked away, the next name was called and the ceremony continued. Julie looked down to admire her new bracelet. As Katie watched Julie, she saw something upsetting. She let go of Ian's hand and tried to get a better view to confirm her suspicions.

As the next selected individual passed, Katie got the good look she needed, and her fears were confirmed.

The bracelets they were giving out to the twenty were blue, not silver.

She nudged Ian to alert him to the color change.

Katie's mind was racing as the ceremony continued. Why would Heron do this? There had to be a reason they would make these twenty people's bracelets a different color.

Finally, well into the ceremony, Ian linked his arm with Katie's, to not only tell her he understood, but also to be supportive. By this time, Avery and Sarah had also apparently noticed the blue bracelets, and each was considering the motive and implications. They weren't sure what to make of it, if anything, and without being able to talk to one another, it was harder to sort out.

Also, with the reporters constantly snapping photos and twenty very excited people receiving their bracelets, there was nothing that could be done. Making a scene would not only ruin these people's moment, but the team had no idea if such a reaction was justified.

So, they just waited as the ceremony continued, and blue bracelet after blue bracelet was given out.

After the last name was called, Malia concluded the ceremony. "I would like to acknowledge Ms. Sullivan, Mr. Callahan, Ms. Jensen, and Ms. Greenbaum for their efforts to make today happen."

As she continued her speech and her praise of Heron's generosity, Katie hung on the line that linked the four them to the distribution of the bracelets—the blue bracelets. What was that going to mean in the future? She had a bad feeling about it.

At the conclusion of the ceremony, Malia and the other Heron employees headed toward Katie, Avery, Sarah, and Ian and acted as escorts as they all exited the room and headed toward the lobby. Not only did this close proximity allow Heron to tie themselves to the four of them and ensured that it would be documented by the media, but it also prevented the four of them from discussing any of their thoughts with one another or the new Phase Two members.

When they reached the foyer, Malia said, "Ms. Sullivan..." She got Katie's attention, and Katie shifted positions within the group to hear what Malia had to say.

Malia continued but began to walk slowly. "I am so sorry for your loss." Malia's pace created some distance between the two of them and the rest of the group. Once the rest of the crowd was out of earshot, Malia's tone changed. "Don't think for one moment that your permitted attendance at this event will be extended to other circumstances. You should walk out those doors, and if you know what is good for you and your friends, you will focus your energy on something else. I expect you will never step foot in these halls again." The look on her face made it all too clear to Katie that this woman was deadly serious.

Katie hurried back to Ian and the group as they were leaving. "Katie, what's wrong?" he asked.

"This was all a mistake. Heron took advantage of our vulnerability due to our pasts and connection to them. They made fools of us, and now those poor people are caught in the middle, and I am sure they will spend the rest of their lives being treated differently due to their blue bracelets. I am just so angry that Heron outsmarted us. They knew that making us feel responsible for the discrimination these people will face would be a far harsher punishment for speaking out than confronting us directly."

"What did Malia say to you?" he asked. "We did everything we could. We have to remember that these twenty people, who desperately wanted a plan, got one, and we helped with that. True, the blue bracelets were unexpected, but we don't know what the consequences of them will be, if any."

Katie kept her silence for the moment.

Chapter 29

As the team was leaving Heron headquarters after the ceremony, Lee Park inched his way up through the group, quickly passing by Avery, so as to not draw attention, and without much more than a pause, he whispered to her, "Article Two, Section Eight."

Avery heard Lee's whisper clearly, although she did not know what to make of it and was caught off guard. Just as she was leaving, she turned back to look at him, but he continued walking quickly and separated himself from the group as they exited.

When the group got outside, Ian was busy ensuring that Katie was okay after what sounded to him like an unpleasant encounter with Malia after the ceremony. Sarah expressed relief that the ceremony and their responsibility for it was over. Avery just didn't feel it appropriate, at least at that very moment, to add to the drama by the questioning that would certainly come from her mentioning what had just happened with Lee to the group. It would have to wait for the time being.

As the car taking them back approached their neighborhood, there was a moment when the group realized that this ceremony marked the end of their journey together. It could be possible they would walk away from this meeting and easily lose contact with each other after spending so much time together to reach a common goal. They all realized this at a similar moment after the conversation had died down a bit, and their enthusiasm settled. Avery broke the tension that was building up as people realized this. No one was sure how to handle the situation.

"We will have to get together soon to make sure we keep in touch." Avery paused a moment. "Why don't we set up a time and place to meet again next week, so we are sure we actually do it? Just maybe not Brio, right?"

They all concurred, understanding that the time spent at that establishment had been filled with angst about a mission they were ready to leave behind.

"Can everyone meet at Ciao Tuesday night at six?" Avery asked.

While the three paused for just a moment as they considered if it would work with their schedules and then looked around at the others, they each responded that they could make that time work. They all thought it was a good idea. As they got out of the car and said their final goodbyes for the evening, they were comforted in knowing that it was not truly goodbye but just a see-you-later.

Once Avery was back at home, she had an opportunity to reflect on the evening and their accomplishments as well as wonder what Lee could have been talking about and why. She was glad that she would have an opportunity to run it past the group when they got together because she really had no idea why Lee would have said something to her or what to make of his very short message "Article Two, Section Eight."

After some days and evenings pondering the possible meaning of Lee's comments, one potential source of the language used by Lee came to Avery. She vaguely remembered receiving a Phase Two manual after her templating, and she started searching through her apartment trying to locate it, which she was certain she had somewhere. Her casual searching turned into scouring every inch of her house, unpacking bins, tossing things out of drawers and thumbing through files. After overturning much of her place, she finally located the document among some miscellaneous school papers. She couldn't resist opening it right then and there, and she plopped down right in the middle of the floor and began flipping through the softbound document looking for any indication of the phrasing used by Lee.

Initially, she was confident that she had found the right document as she saw similar language, a Section Two. Maybe she could find an item Eight within that, but as she spent more time trying to decipher Lee's message and match it to the document in her possession, the more she became frustrated and started to think that she may be searching down the wrong path. Frustrated, she set the manual down and gave thanks that she would have an opportunity to discuss the situation with the group tomorrow. She was coming up short, and she was hopeful that the team could provide some insight. Avery was ready to share this conundrum with the group in order to get to the bottom of the mystery but also to just have someone to talk to about all that had been going through her mind, over the past few days, since the ceremony and Lee's puzzling remark.

Avery tried to get this puzzle out of her mind and wait for the team's insight the following evening, but she had a restless night's sleep and trouble doing anything else until it was time for the group to meet at Ciao.

Her desire to see the group and hear their thoughts caused Avery to arrive early to Ciao. As the remaining three arrived, each one commented on and questioned Avery's uncharacteristically early arrival.

Last to get there was Sarah, who felt perfectly comfortable making light of the situation at Avery's expense. "Avery! Are you feeling okay? Is everything all right?"

"All right, all right, everyone," Avery said, taking the remarks in stride. After a short pause, she added, "Actually, I do have something I wanted to discuss with the group."

The group was listening, but there was a collective sigh from them. They could tell that what she had to say was serious. After all, they had been through, they were hoping for a little peace and a normal meal with cordial conversation.

Avery explained to the group what had happened when she and Lee were leaving Heron after the ceremony last week. She had tried to decipher what he could have been trying to tell her, but so far, she had not been unable to make heads nor tails of it. She was hoping for more information as well as help and ideas from the group. "Can anybody think of anything that Lee could have meant by that?"

The group listened intently, but they appeared somewhat skeptical. "Are you sure you heard him correctly?" Sarah asked. "Are you positive he was talking to you?"

Her question annoyed Avery because she was definitely sure she knew what she heard and that Lee was trying to tell her something. Why else had she been thinking about it for days on end and racking her brain, trying to figure out what he could have been trying to tell them? Most certainly, she wouldn't have bothered the group with it unless she was sure.

"Yes, I'm sure," Avery said firmly.

Trying to diffuse the bit of tension that had built up during the time the others had questioned Avery, Katie said, "Okay, we believe you. We just wanted to be sure. We'll all be brainstorming to try to think about what that could have meant. We'll be sure to tell you any ideas that we have." As Katie said this, she looked around for reassurance from Ian and Sarah to be sure they would agree with her proposal to Avery.

"Of course," Ian said.

"You know I have your back," Sarah added, comforting Avery somewhat.

Avery felt some solace in knowing that the group not only knew about the situation but that there were three more brains helping to figure this thing out. Even if the group didn't seem quite as invested in the situation or seem to feel the same urgency as Avery felt, she was confident that they would follow through in thinking about it and letting her know if something came to them. She did her best to not fill the rest of the group's conversations with all of her farfetched ideas of what Lee could have meant, and she tried to enjoy the time catching up with the group and hearing what they had been up to over the last week and to have a somewhat normal conversation. This was something they hadn't been able to have during much of the time they had all known each other.

The morning after the group get-together at Ciao, Avery received a call from Ian. "Have you tried looking at the Phase Two contract?" he asked.

"Oh my gosh, No." Avery realized this was an oversight on her part. "That is a good idea. Thanks for taking the time to think about it."

"Of course. Do you know where your copy is?"

"No, but I am going to go find it right now. I will get back to you if I find anything. Actually, I'll get back to you either way. Thank you so much, Ian."

Avery was pretty sure that the document was something she received electronically, but she was not the most organized person, and so, sifting through her emails and their corresponding attachments was not an easy task. Nevertheless, she started right away, and after a few searches of her email using key words such as "Heron" and "Contract," she was able to locate a document she had signed electronically.

Her initial excitement about locating the document that Ian had suggested she review was overshadowed by a feeling of intimidation mixed with a little defeat as she realized how incredibly long the document was and the complexity of the language it contained. She was sure that she hadn't even attempted to read any part of the document when they sent it over.

She had just clicked "Agree with terms" prior to digitally signing it. She felt at a loss of how to tackle the document to search for the language quoted by Lee. She forwarded the email and accompanying document to Ian in hopes that his expertise as a journalist might somehow provide him with the skills to decipher what she could not.

Ian, I was excited about your suggestion, and I was able to locate the Phase Two contract, but I have no idea how to search this type of document. Is there any way you can help me?

Shortly after sending her email, Avery received a response.

No problem. When I have a minute, I will look through it. Can you remind me exactly what Lee said to you?

Article 2, Section 8, Avery responded.

Later that day Avery received a call from Ian. She hadn't anticipated that Ian would work so quickly, or that he would contact her via phone with his findings.

"Hey," he said in such a serious tone that he got her attention. "I think I found what you were looking for. Are you near a computer?"

"I can be."

"I just sent you the language in the contract under Article Two, Section Eight. Avery, this was not easy to find. It was buried deep in this document among other seemingly innocuous language."

Avery opened her computer and read the email from Ian while he waited.

People will be transitioned into Phase Two on a space-available basis, and in the event of a waiting list, the Plans will be awarded to the individuals in order, based on their Heron rating.

"Um, what the heck is this? What is a Heron rating?" Avery's mind was racing.

Ian had had more time to process and think about the implications of this sentence and perhaps why Lee had said this to Avery as they were leaving the ceremony. "Avery, while I am no legal expert, this language seems to give Heron the ability to selectively transition only individuals of their choosing into Phase Two regardless of who has paid for a plan."

"What? This company is absolutely insane." Then it dawned on Avery. "Oh my gosh, they have no intention of giving the twenty individuals from the ceremony a plan, do they? They are just going to use this contract language to do whatever they want."

"I think that may be the case," Ian said. "And this is what Lee was trying to tell you."

"This company's unbelievable. We can't let this go."

"I'm not sure there's much we can do."

"Well, I am certainly not going to sit around, especially because I know Heron's intent and I understand what those twenty people believe they are getting."

Avery was ready to move on and try to think about what to do with this information. She wrapped things up with Ian for the time being. "Thank you so much for your help finding that language. I'll call you soon."

"Okay, Avery. Don't do anything crazy."

Immediately following her call with Ian, she placed a call to Reuben.

"Wasn't that ceremony delightful?" he asked. "It must feel wonderful to have been instrumental in making that happen for those people. The impact you have made on them in invaluable."

Avery groaned before saying, "I thought so, but once again this company is not what it appears to be."

Reuben's frustration was palpable almost immediately. He felt as if he had really gone out on a limb for Avery and her friends, and, that after the ceremony, they could all move on, but he could see now that Avery was caught up again. Before he could ask for clarification, Avery continued.

"Have you read the contract?"

"What contract?"

"The Phase Two contract?"

"No, but surely my lawyers have."

"Well, there is some concerning language that basically negates the plans that they just gave out and probably other contracts too."

"Are you sure you aren't reading too much into this or maybe over-reacting a little?" Reuben asked carefully.

"No, Reuben, this is serious!"

"What part specifically concerns you?"

"This part called Article Two, Section Eight. It basically states that they don't have to give plans to people they don't want to."

"Okay, Avery, I'm sure that there's a reasonable interpretation for the language you're referring to."

"I seriously doubt it. I can't believe that you deal with these people."

Reuben let the comment pass and continued, "I'll look into it and, hopefully, we can get this sorted out. Would that make you happy?"

"Yes, as a matter of fact, it would," Avery said.

She was frustrated with Reuben's skepticism, but at the same time, she was thankful for his willingness to check it out, because she really didn't have anywhere else to turn at this point.

Chapter 30

After hanging up with Avery, Reuben decided to make a call to Heron. He figured it was nothing serious, and he might as well deal with it quickly and then calm Avery down.

Malia at Heron listened to her messages and heard the following, "Malia, this is Reuben from Theta Technologies, and I am calling on behalf of my daughter Avery. She has approached me with a concern regarding some language she claims is in Article Two, Section Eight of the Phase Two contracts. I have assured her that it is nothing but have promised to follow up with you to get clarification on this Section. Please return my call regarding this concern as soon as possible."

As Malia was listening to the message, her blood began to boil. First of all, how was anyone, let alone this young woman, able to find the Article Two, Section Eight language? Second of all, she thought they had dealt with this meddling from Avery and the others, and third of all, this had to be stopped.

Malia slammed down the phone and immediately paged Tyson to come to her office.

Tyson arrived and entered somewhat timidly. He knocked and peeked his head in prior to entering her office to ensure that he did not interrupt anything, as well as see what he was walking into.

"You needed something? What can I do for you?" he asked.

Malia started to provide far more information than necessary and certainly more detail than was typical for her comments, assuredly due to her high level of irritation. "Yes. Avery Jensen is stirring the pot yet again."

"Do you have a plan?" Tyson asked.

Malia continued without answering his question directly, "She has to be stopped. She is meddling in our business, and because of her ties to Theta, she could become a real problem for us, if we don't take care of this right now."

Tyson waited for Malia's instructions, which he could tell were coming.

"Please contact Ms. Jensen and set up an appointment. We are going to have to implement the alteration protocol with her."

Tyson was shocked, but he knew better than to question her authority.

"Yes, ma'am," he replied.

"Alert Warren so he can prepare the necessary template for her appointment and contact Ms. Jensen to set up her appointment as soon as possible. Update me immediately once you have made contact with her regarding the appointment."

"What shall I tell her the appointment is for?"

"I am sure you will figure out something," Malia said.

Tyson took that reply as his cue to exit. When he reached his desk, he called Warren to set the wheels in motion.

"Warren, I need to start an alteration protocol for Ms. Jensen."

"An alteration protocol for Ms. Jensen?" he repeated.

"Yes. Right away."

Warren hung up.

Tyson dialed Ms. Jensen.

"Ms. Jensen. This is Tyson at Heron."

Avery audibly groaned and then said, "Yes?"

"I have been alerted that we need to do a routine update to your template. Is there a time in the next few days when you could come in? It shouldn't take long."

Avery thought for a quick moment because she really had little concern about maintaining her Phase Two plan or template. She however also saw an opportunity to speak her mind to Heron if she had a chance to get in Heron in person. She knew Reuben was working on it, but she thought that it wouldn't hurt for her to have another option as well.

"I could do Friday."

Tyson was pleased that it was not as challenging as he had anticipated to get Avery to come in. "We can absolutely make that work. What time is best for you?"

"Around four in the afternoon?"

"We will see you then, Ms. Jensen."

Both Avery and Tyson hung up satisfied. Avery felt good knowing that she would have an opportunity to speak to someone at Heron regardless of what happened to Reuben's work.

Avery felt she should let Ian know she had this appointment because he had helped her with the contract language. She called Ian's line but got his voicemail, "Ian, I just wanted to say thank you so much for your help with the contract language, and I have contacted Reuben. He is looking into this issue. I have an appointment with Heron on Friday, and I plan to talk to them myself. I have a super busy day of classes and study sessions on Friday, but I am headed there after work at four o'clock. I will let you know how it goes. Thanks again,"

When her appointment came, she arrived at Heron. She walked into the building with a sense of authority, something she had never before displayed at the Heron offices. In the past, Avery had found the Heron offices somewhat intimidating. The grandiose building, the formality of the greeting, and frankly, the nature of their business had made her feel somewhat meek in the past, but today she felt different. She had something to prove, and she didn't plan to be intimidated.

As Avery took firm and quick step after firm and quick step into the Heron lobby, as expected, Malia walked out to greet her. As Malia approached, Avery mentally prepared her words to immediately give Malia a piece of her mind.

"Malia, I have—" Avery began.

"Avery Jensen! Delightful to see you." Malia said, cutting her off. Without a pause, Malia put her hand around Avery's back and continued to speak while she directed her forward. "I see you have a routine template updating appointment today. I will take you over to Warren, who is ready for you. This should take no time at all."

Before Avery could even try again to discuss her concerns with Malia, they had reached Warren, who was waiting at the door.

"Warren. Ms. Jensen is here for her appointment." Malia said handing Avery off.

"I had something important I wanted to discuss with you," Avery said.

"I would be more than happy to meet with you following your appointment."

Malia's cordial response and willingness to meet

with her following the appointment confused Avery, and she was at a loss for words. Still, after the appointment was better than nothing.

Warren walked Avery into the room. Once inside, he gave her the same information about changing clothes that she had heard at her initial templating. This was necessary because her template was being updated.

Warren stepped out of the main portion of the templating room and closed a curtain door behind him to give Avery privacy as she changed into the paper robe. Warren could see that Malia was by the door, and it appeared as if she wanted a word with him. He approached Malia, who said in a firm whisper, "Warren, we need to get this taken care of seamlessly and as soon as possible."

Leaning in, Warren quietly replied, "It should not be a problem. I have the adjusted template ready to go, and once she is sedated, her displeasure with Heron should be eradicated in a matter of moments."

"Good." Malia nodded. "Let me know as soon as you have finished."

Chapter 31

Friday Lee Park came into work as usual and checked his agenda. He knew he needed to drop by a few offices to check on network connections, and he was prepared for a fairly routine shift. As he checked his email, he saw a work order with both urgent and confidential notifications from Malia. Without even having to read the work order further, Lee Park knew what to expect. He had seen only one other work order project marked *urgent and confidential* during his time at Heron. He felt sick as he opened the work order and saw the words, "Ensure the system in room one is ready for an alteration protocol with Ms. Avery Jensen. Seamless operation is essential." He also saw a notification that the work order status had already been marked as complete.

While he had seen the protocol a few times before, he hadn't personally met any individual for whom Heron planned to adjust the template in order to benefit the company.

Lee slipped out of the office and down the hall, where he swiped a key card on a door. He quickly looked around, and when he saw that all was clear, he ducked into the storage room. He pulled out his phone and dialed Avery's number. He never expected to do that after their lunch meeting, but he had to try to get in contact with her. He nervously waited as the phone rang and eventually went to voicemail. He knew now that he couldn't leave a message. He already was putting himself at too much risk just making the call, and he was certainly not comfortable being on record going against Heron. He hung up and racked his brain about what to do next. He decided to try calling Katie. Heron was about to send Avery into Phase Two with an altered template without her knowledge, but he didn't anticipate that Katie would be skeptical of his assertion. He was still tucked away in the dark, tiny room when he dialed her.

Once she answered, Lee responded in a firm voice just above a whisper. "Katie. It's Lee Park. From Heron."

Katie was caught off guard.

"Lee?"

"Yes. Do you remember me?"

"Of course. Are you okay? I can hardly hear you."

"Yes, Katie, listen carefully."

Lee's words and tone of voice got Katie's attention and put her on edge.

Lee continued, "Avery is on the schedule here at Heron today for an alteration protocol."

"Okay?" Katie said. She was confused, and she didn't know what an alteration protocol was. She did know that Avery had a current Phase Two plan with Heron.

"Katie, this is serious. Heron is having Avery come in for what she thinks is a routine template update. During the appointment, they will bring about her initial departure and then send her into Phase Two, without her permission or knowledge, with a new adjusted template that will eliminate her displeasure with Heron."

"What?"

"I don't have time to explain all the details, Katie, but if you want to do something to help, you are going to have to work fast. Avery will be here soon. Her appointment is at four p.m. I don't know what Avery did to prompt this type of action from Heron, but they are not known for their understanding, kindness, compassion, or fairness."

"What are you talking about?"

"I have to go." Lee quickly ended the call and slipped back into the hall and back to work. He was on edge, but he had done what he could. It was in Katie's hands now. For Avery's sake, he hoped she acted quickly.

After Lee hung up, Katie was momentarily stunned. She hadn't realized it, but over the course of the time the group had been working together, she had grown so fond of Avery that she was extremely protective of her. Having lost her daughter, Katie had transferred some of her mothering instincts and tendencies to Avery. When she finally pulled herself together, her first instinct was to call Ian. When he didn't answer, she started to lose hope. She didn't know what to do. She didn't understand what was happening or how to make it stop, but she knew she didn't have much time. She spoke out loud in order to try to pull herself together. "Katie, you can do this. Avery needs you. You can do this. Think. Think. Think."

Then, it came to her. She had to get in contact with Reuben. Knowing that she didn't have much time, she grabbed her coat and purse, headed to her car, and drove directly to Theta Technologies. When she arrived, her typical adherence to convention was out the window. She walked directly past the guard at his station in the lobby and headed directly toward the elevators without pausing. As she made her way past the station, the guard looked up, made the assumption that she must belong where she was because she was walking with such confidence, and he simply said "Ma'am? Can I alert someone that you are on your way?"

Katie cracked a tiny smile, pleased with herself. "No," she said in her most confident tone. "That won't be necessary."

The guard appeared uneasy and momentarily wondered if he should track her down and see that she properly checked in. At the same time, he didn't dare offend any important person here to visit Mr. Wilkins. He decided to watch on the security cameras as she continued into the elevator.

Katie entered the elevator and looked at the button selections unsure of what to press. She hadn't considered on which floor to find Reuben. There was no going back to the guard now, so she hoped for the best and selected the top floor.

When the guard saw Katie exit at Reuben's floor, he watched even more carefully.

Katie exited the elevator and found herself directly in front of two large wooden doors. As she looked to the side of the doors, she was relieved to see a prominent name placard displaying "Reuben Wilkins, CEO." She took a deep breath, opened the doors, and walked in.

The guard watching on the cameras returned to his work. He was feeling confident that there wasn't anything to worry about, because he didn't see anything alarming in the surveillance video.

Immediately when she opened the doors, she started in, as she wasn't sure how much time she would have before Reuben or the guard took some sort of action. "Mr. Wilkins. I am a friend of Avery's, and she is in trouble."

Reuben was already standing behind his desk ready to object to her arrival. Momentarily ignoring her comments, he said, "How did you get in here?"

Katie continued, "Reuben, this is serious. Avery is in major trouble. Heron is planning to take her out and transition her to Phase Two with an altered template that will eradicate her opposition to Heron."

Reuben was clearly irritated. "Ma'am, Katie, was it? Please have a seat. I need to make a phone call."

Grateful to have his attention, Katie sat down. Reuben picked up his phone and dialed the guard station. "Derek, can you please send someone up to my office. I have a Ms. Katie up here."

It wasn't necessary for Mr. Wilkens to say any more for Derek to understand that the woman who had just walked by earlier was not a guest Reuben was expecting or wanted.

"Right away, sir," Derek said hoping to redeem himself for allowing the women to pass by him in the first place.

Reuben redirected his attention to Katie. "I understand you are a friend of Avery, but like her, you have quite an imagination. I am sure you have the best of intentions, but I cannot imagine that Heron is planning to, as you say, 'take Avery out.'"

Desperate, Katie said, "I understand it sounds crazy, and I probably would have thought I was insane myself prior to my experiences with Heron, but regardless of what you think, this is Avery we're talking about. They are going to not only put her in Phase Two, which will only give ten years to live, but they are going to alter who she is for the remainder of her life."

"Where are you getting this information?"

Katie was nervous to jeopardize Lee Park by giving his name to Reuben after all Lee had risked for the group and most recently for Avery. "A worker at Heron just alerted me about Avery's appointment and Heron's intentions."

"I need a name," Reuben pressed further.

Katie held her ground hoping that it wouldn't further jeopardize Avery's safety. "I cannot provide you the name, but I promise you this person can be trusted." She continued to fear that she was on the brink of either convincing or losing Reuben. "Reuben, this is your daughter. Please come with me to Heron right now to check it out. Maybe you are right, and it will turn out to be nothing, but what if I am right and Avery is in trouble, and we don't do anything? I know I couldn't live with that. I promise that if it turns out to be nothing, I will be out of your hair immediately."

Reuben sighed. "I will go, but I'm doing so only to show you that all this is just routine at Heron. Avery is not in danger, and you and Avery both need to stop with this nonsense."

As they exited Reuben's office, the guard was waiting.

"Please have someone bring a car around so that Ms. Katie and I can head to Heron," Reuben told him.

"Yes, sir," the guard replied.

As Katie and Reuben walked into the elevator, the guard made the call regarding the car from his walkie-talkie.

Katie and Reuben got into the car and soon arrived at Heron. Katie entered Heron with the same confidence with which she entered Theta Technologies, but this time she was bolstered by that fact that Reuben Wilkens was by her side, and she was far more certain that she would not be questioned.

Nevertheless, she was displaying more confidence than was typical.

Before Reuben and Malia had a chance to exchange pleasantries, Katie demanded, "Where's Avery?"

Malia remained calm. "Welcome, Mr. Wilkens. I was not aware that you knew Ms. Sullivan," she said, expressing disdain for Katie in her tone of voice.

Reuben responded diplomatically. "We were just recently acquainted."

Katie, who was growing impatient, demanded again, "Where is Avery?"

"Ms. Sullivan, Avery is just going in for in a routine template update. You are welcome to wait here for her. It shouldn't be long."

"That seems reasonable," Reuben responded.

Katie cut him off, "That is not acceptable. We need to speak to her immediately."

Malia worked to maintain her composure and said, "Ms. Sullivan, I will go check on her and be back with you shortly."

Malia walked away briskly, and when she reached the end of the corridor, she turned, entered a room, and immediately picked up a phone. "Warren, this is Malia. We may have a problem. How far along are you?"

"Ms. Jensen has just returned, and we are ready to get started."

"Get on with it then!" Malia said.

Chapter 32

As Avery was getting changed, she could hear the quiet but insistent whisperings of Warren and someone she assumed was Malia. She didn't, however, think much of it, and she figured that there was some important Heron business they were discussing. Avery was looking forward to her own discussion with Malia of some very important business following her appointment. Just as she had nearly finished putting on the paper robe and was close to being ready to emerge from behind the curtain, Avery heard yet another disturbance outside the room. This time it was what sounded like a disgruntled Heron employee. Although she could not make out exactly what they were saying from the confines of her room, she could tell that the person was a very agitated female.

While the earlier conversation between Malia and Warren did not get much notice from Avery, this outburst unnerved her. She hesitated behind the curtain and continued to listen. When she felt that things had settled a bit, she emerged from behind the curtain in her paper gown. Just as she was exiting the privacy area, she heard the phone in the room ring. Warren signaled to her that he was going to grab it. Avery clearly overheard Warren saying, "Ms. Jensen has just returned, and we are ready to get started."

Warren headed back to Avery whose face was clearly showing some skepticism and interest in what was going on in the Heron building. "I am so sorry, Ms. Jensen," he said. "That was just a routine call confirming that we are on schedule here and that we can go ahead with your update."

Avery nodded, but she still had a strange feeling.

"If you could just sit up on the table, as you did at your initial template appointment, we will give you a sedative, and once you are out, we will do the necessary update, and before you know it, you will be alert again and back to life as usual."

As Avery walked toward the table to lie down and receive the sedative, she once again heard the voice of an agitated female coming from outside the room. Because she was closer to the door than she was before, she could make out just slightly more.

"…not okay…Where is she?"

Avery looked at Warren. "What is happening out there? Is everything all right? That woman sounds very upset."

"I am sure everything is fine. As you can imagine, due to the nature of the business, Heron has encounters with some passionate people."

"Right. I see."

Avery, somewhat reluctantly, got herself up on the table, and Warren and his team began to prep her for the administration of the sedative.

"Avery, are you in here?"

"What? Is that you, Katie?" Avery began to sit up at the table. The template team surrounding her moved closer. Avery looked around at the team members. "Was that person calling for me?" she asked as she started to get up off the table.

The team members closed in on the table, and the two members nearest the middle of the table grabbed her arm with one hand and with the other pressed her back down. As they did, Warren said, "Ms. Jensen, please lie back. We have a procedure we need to follow."

"What are you doing?" Avery demanded.

"Remain calm, Ms. Jensen. This will all be over soon."

This caused Avery to push harder against the team members as she tried to move her feet and arms. She began to realize she was being restrained.

"Katie!" she yelled out, hoping that it was, in fact, Katie she heard behind the door.

The template team continued to hold her down, and as the team held her, they also worked her into arm and leg restraints attached to the table. The restraints prevented her from being able to get off the table, but they did not prevent her from writhing around.

"Katie! I'm in here!" she shouted.

"Hold her down," Warren said. "I need her still to be able to do this."

Avery continued to yell out to Katie, but within minutes, she could sense the sedative they managed to give her was setting in, and her muscles weren't allowing her to fight with the same strength.

While they hadn't been able to give her a full dose of sedative due to her writhing, they were convinced it was enough to calm her down. The team backed away somewhat, as if knowing that they just had to wait until they could proceed with the procedure.

Katie was frustrated with both Reuben and Malia. She was irritated that Reuben did not seem concerned about Avery's safety and also that Malia was not taking them to see Avery immediately.

When Malia walked away after telling her she "would check on Avery," Katie waited only a few beats before impatiently looking at Reuben, who seemed more than content waiting for Malia's return, and then started walking farther into Heron headquarters and heading toward some doors behind which she hoped that she would find Avery.

She attempted to open the door by jostling the handle, only to find it locked. She knocked and called out, "Avery, are you in there?" Then she moved onto the next door and began the same actions. After that door, she found herself face to face with Malia who clearly was not happy that Katie had decided to take finding Avery into her own hands.

"Ms. Sullivan!" Malia started to scold Katie as Reuben slowly approached. This caused Malia to change her tone somewhat as she continued, "I told you that Avery is here for a routine template update and that I would check on her and get back with you."

"We need to see her immediately. This is not okay. Where is she?" Katie said. Then she knocked again defiantly. "Avery, are you in here?"

"Ms. Sullivan, that is quite enough!" Malia turned to Reuben. "Avery is certainly fine," she said. "There's nothing to worry about, and just as soon as the procedure is over, the two of you can see her."

"No," Katie said.

Malia ignored her and addressed Reuben. "If you could just follow me to the lobby—"

"Katie! Katie, help!"

Both Reuben and Katie turned to one another as they both heard the cry from behind a door nearby. Katie ran toward the voice.

"Ms. Sullivan! You are not permitted in that area!"

Katie continued, but she could see that she soon would be met by guards preventing any further progress toward the voice.

Katie turned to Reuben, "Reuben, that was Avery! Calling out for help! Surely now you have to believe something is going on. We have to do something."

Reuben, who up until this point had been passive, said in a firm voice, "Malia, you will need to permit Katie and me to pass to the templating suites."

"Reuben, it is only authorized personnel beyond this point."

Reuben, who was not accustomed to being told no, simply walked past Malia. "In that case, today, we need to be authorized personnel."

"Katie! I'm in here!" the voice called out again.

Katie, pleased with her ability to snap Reuben into reality, started running toward the voice, "Reuben, I think it was coming from here."

Before opening the door, she looked quickly at Reuben, took in some air, let out a deep breath, and with that, she opened the door. In front of her, down a short flight of stairs, she saw Avery surrounded by a team of templaters. She could clearly see that Avery was resisting the restraints on the table. As she looked down, she saw the helplessness in Avery's eyes.

"What is going on here?" Katie demanded as she walked closer.

"Ma'am," Warren replied, confused by the intrusion, "this is just a routine template update."

As Katie approached the table, she could clearly see that Avery was restrained. "This does not look routine! Release her from these restraints immediately!" Katie got closer, leaned in, and asked Avery, "Are you all right?"

Avery was getting weaker, but she managed to say in a broken voice, "I—I—heard them saying something about an altered template."

Katie repeated loudly what she had heard Avery say. It was directed to everyone but in particular to Reuben. "I told you! They are going to give her an altered template! She heard it herself!"

Reuben, who had tried to remain as neutral as possible until this point because of his ties to both Avery and Heron, realized that Avery was in danger, and he certainly couldn't stand by any longer. After Katie's declaration, and, as he looked at the faces of both Malia and Warren, he could see from their expressions that it was true.

"Katie, I apologize, I didn't want to believe you. I am thankful you brought me here." He turned to Malia and Warren. "We demand you release Avery, or you will no longer have any association with Theta Technologies or have our financial support. I will not tolerate these actions!"

Malia could see that there was no other way out of this situation. They needed to preserve their crucial relationship with Theta Technologies. They could not be seen to be taking drastic action against Avery with this audience. If they willingly let Avery go now, they would hopefully be able to maintain the relationship with Theta with little damage to the Heron image.

Malia gave a nod to indicate to Warren that they were going to comply. Warren shrugged and reached down to unbuckle the restraints. As Avery was released, Katie embraced her, supported her as she got off the table, and helped her to her feet. She helped Avery back to the room with her clothes and assisted her in getting dressed.

As Katie walked Avery to the door of the room past Warren and Malia, she gave them a stern look as she passed by and continued straight toward the exit of Heron. As they walked out of the Heron headquarters arm in arm, supporting one another, Avery said, "I'm kind of dizzy. Hold onto me, please."

"I've got you." Tears filled Katie's eyes, and she clung even more tightly to this beautiful child. "I've got you, and it's going to be all right."

End

About the Author

Sandra Sikonia lives in the Pacific Northwest with her husband and daughter where she is a high school teacher. She loves taking advantage of all that the great outdoors has to offer by spending time in the mountains, skiing and biking, on the water, paddle boarding, and in the woods, hiking and camping.

www.ingramcontent.com/pod-product-compliance
Lightning Source LLC
Chambersburg PA
CBHW061028120726
47910CB00006B/2153